Barren Earth

Stephen Alexander North and Eric S. Brown

Stephen Alexander North

Without Dr. Michael West, I doubt this book would exist. We knew him as 'Doc', short for Doctor Pus. His publishing company, The Library of the Living Dead (later Twisted Press), brought many people together that may have otherwise never met. Eric S. Brown is one of those people I may never have known, let alone wrote a book with. I'm glad I had the pleasure of meeting him once at a Horror Realm Convention in Pittsburgh. He is hard-working, a devoted family man, and a friend. Strangely enough, we both worked for the same company, besides being horror/sci-fi writers. Anyway, I hated to see this book out of print for so long. Thank you, Doc, Eric, and all the good librarians! -SAN

"To know your Enemy, you must become your Enemy." — Sun Tzu

"We do not merely destroy our enemies; we change them." — George Orwell, 1984

Contents

Chapter 1

2119 A.D.   BOOK ONE

The three people on the bridge sat at their posts, still tense, even though the alarm klaxon was finally silent. A kilometer away, the vast bulky remains of an alien warship drifted alongside theirs.

"Unknown vessel, this is Terran Federation Ship *Cormorant* requesting permission to board. Please identify yourself. "

The communications officer repeated the phrases for a fifth time, and then paused a moment to lick his dry lips.

"Might as well give it up, Jackson. They won't answer. It's a derelict," said the captain.

The younger man, Lt. Commander Neil Jackson, looked up from his console. "I know, sir, but we finally find evidence of other life, only to discover they're dead."

The captain nodded. "Worse to discover that they had a violent end." The image filling the viewscreen was too large at their current distance to see the entire thing. Magnification would have to be reduced. Huge, jagged holes ran the length and breadth of the other ship.

"Maybe there is life, but it's just shielded from our sensors?"

The third person, Ensign Mary Powers, pointed to the strategic screen, just left of the main tactical display. She was small-framed,

1

with average looks but a head of wavy, blonde hair. "There's a chance, Commander Jackson. Sensors have picked up a minor power reading. Maybe an emergency generator. Not from the engines. Also, the second planet has a habitable atmosphere, and there is a shielded facility on the second continent."

"And I'm picking up a transmission, sir!" said Jackson.

"A transmission, you say?" asked the captain.

"Yes, sir, but nothing intelligible so far through Rashid's AI, just a repeating sequence."

"Very well. Powers, lay in a course to orbit the planet."

"Course set, Captain. Power readings are dropping from the facility. A planetary shield either just lowered or failed. Still no signs of biological life beyond plants and fauna. The planet has a breathable atmosphere with gravity to our standards."

"What are the odds of that, eh?" The captain cocked his right elbow on the armrest of the chair and rested his chin in his cupped palm. He looked forty, but was well past fifty years old, with short-cropped gray hair, and a patrician, Roman-look to him. He looked anything but happy at this development. "Perhaps a robotic intelligence remains. We appear to have an invitation to visit."

"We are within shuttle range now, Captain."

"Very well..." he said, then trailed off.

"Want me to put together a landing team, sir?" asked Jackson, looking at the older man.

"Yes. This entire system feels dead... Can't you feel it? Like we're violating a tomb, but we must find out what happened here. Go ahead, put together a team. Use bio-suits just in case, and take some Marines."

"Yes, sir," Jackson replied, already on his feet.

Chapter 2

JACKSON

"*Cormorant*, are you getting the feed of this?" Jackson asked while settling the shuttle gently on a wide, tiled palazzo. They landed on the edge of a large ruined city complex bordered on three sides by impenetrable jungle and on the fourth, southern side, by a large circular bay. "I'm sending Sergeant Marks and Private Crane out first, then the rest of us will follow."

"Reading you loud and clear, and visuals are good, Commander," said the voice of Ensign Powers. "Captain wants you to investigate the source of transmission in a large temple two clicks directly north of your position."

"Affirmative, proceeding, out."

Jackson watched from the pilot's seat as the figures of Marks and Crane emerged from the airlock and ran toward a low, crumbling stone wall that surrounded their landing zone.

Marks spoke, "All clear Commander. Nothing moving out here. But I'd swear we're being watched."

"Very good, Sergeant. Stay alert. The rest of us are coming."

Jackson lifted himself up and out of the cockpit and onto the narrow slice of deck that separated the pilot seat from the co-pilot/navigator's seat. It only took two steps to reach the ladder down into the passenger area, where Warrant Officer Leila Tran waited for him with the hood of her bio-suit pulled down. All the others were already outside.

"Here's your machine pistol, sir," she said with her faint French-accented English.

"Thanks," he said, unable to meet his lover's frank gaze. She only hid her feelings for him when others were around. He couldn't get used to her loving him so much.

"You will be careful, Neil?"

"Yes, Leila, and be ready to come get us if something happens."

He pulled her to his chest, inhaled the scent of her long, black hair, and kissed her. He put all the pent-up emotion he'd held back for the last day or so into it, and, a moment or two later, they parted.

"See you," he murmured into her ear."

Chapter 3

CRANE

They advanced in a long, spread out, V-shaped formation across a field of knee-high grass. A little breeze blew from the south, carrying with it a strange half-familiar scent of the sea. Each of them held a weapon, wore a protective suit that covered them from head to toe, and a helmet with a solar-sensitive visor. The marines wore armor as part of their normal load out.

Crane walked farther out in front of the others, grumbling to himself. His finger fidgeted on the trigger guard of his short, stubby submachine gun. He was careful not to broadcast to anyone else, but felt the need to vent. Not even twenty feet away, five awkward-looking birds perched on top of the overturned wreck of a tracked vehicle.

Looked military, like a personnel carrier, but was little more than a shell now. None of the birds stirred. "Damn lazy things," Crane muttered, "must be the local version of vultures."

"You got that right," said someone nearby.

"Oh, it's you, Sola," he said to the small, tanned brown-haired woman a few feet away. She was recording the birds with her All-One, a scanner, recorder and sampling device about the size of a medium-sized purse. Her weapon was now slung over her shoulder. "Why did you break formation?"

"I'm a researcher," she replied, without turning around. "You do your job and I'll do mine."

"Bitch."

That one got her to turn around. Emotion flushed her delicate, beautiful little face. *Probably rage.*

"I heard that, Crane."

"Your lack of discipline will get us killed."

"What is going on here?" thundered the voice of Sergeant Marks. He stopped walking right next to the tiny woman, forcing her to look up. The soldier was over a foot taller than her, five feet and a few inches. He pointed his assault rifle at the birds.

"Nothing Sergeant," Sola answered. "I just want to check out the wrecked vehicle. Get some shots of the local fauna."

Marks glared at her. "Use a little common sense, will you, Doctor? Those things are most likely predators. We're too close to them now."

She held up a hand. "You win, Sergeant. I don't have the energy to argue with you. Let's skip it, eh?"

Marks nodded. "And get back to your place in the formation or I'll send you back to the shuttle."

Both men waited until she took her place, then Marks re-opened the radio channel, "Go ahead, Crane, we don't have all day."

There wasn't a cloud in the sky as the breeze died away to nothing. The sun dominated the blasted landscape, and the ruins of the dead city sprawling before them for kilometers. Six people, five straight-backed, and one, hunched and misshapen, toiled the last steps to the top of a small hill and stopped. A line of temples were the closest intact structures to them.

"This sun is torturing me, Botts," complained the tallest, a man named Tircek. Sweat was pouring off the man's raw-boned frame, staining his suit.

The hunchbacked man beside him nodded. "Feels like we've been walking for hours. Not used to heat anymore. I wish we could take these damned suits off."

"I wish you'd both stop complaining," said Sola. "Besides, it looks like we have found civilization."

"Civilization?" muttered the hunchbacked man. "All I see is an open-aired tomb. Not a living soul down there, I bet."

"Probably plenty of things, though," Crane whispered to himself. He was close enough to the target structure to notice details. Much of the pyramid-shaped building was in ruins and sheathed with some sort of vine-like growth. Steps were visible ascending the west side of the building, but his orders were to make for the door that stood open at the base.

Crane thought: *The last thing I want to do is go underground, much rather climb.*

He looked up at the violet-hued sky. The sun looked bigger than Sol. *I'm sure if I asked Tircek, he'd know if it was.*

"Stop beside the door, Crane," said Commander Jackson through his ear bud. "Wait for Marks to join you, then keep going."

"Yes sir," he answered, and noticed what looked like bones at the edge of the ramp that led down beneath the building. "Sir, I think I've found bones. No doubt about it, actually. There's a humanoid skull."

More bones were scattered in the grass and had a scorched look. *What else could they be?*

"Wait for the rest of us, then."

Moments later, they had a circular perimeter set up, and Jackson joined Crane where he found the bones. Both of them squatted in the grass, and Crane showed him the skull. Most of the cranium looked intact, and there were two holes where eye sockets should be. There was a jagged row of teeth, but the lower jaw and chin were missing.

"What are the odds, Commander?" Crane asked.

"Impossible. These bones are ancient. None of our ships have been here before."

Jackson lifted the skull with his gloved right hand and placed it in a small opaque specimen bag. "Here Tircek, add this to your pack."

Tircek stepped up. He handed Crane his shotgun. "Hold this a moment, will you?" He then took off his backpack. Jackson gave him the skull. A minute or two later, he had everything stowed. He pulled the backpack on and took his shotgun back.

Guy's hands are huge. He could easily palm a basketball. Hell, maybe even a bowling ball!

"Want me to take point again, sir?" Crane asked. Jackson's visor was clear as a glass of water. The sky was getting darker.

"Yeah," Jackson said, and their eyes met briefly. "Do that."

Crane felt a chill then. It traveled up his arms and raised the hair on the back of his neck. He made himself stand up and place his boots on the strange, spongy surface of the ramp. He took three steps down and flicked on his helmet light. The walls had a raw fleshy look to them, complete with rocky strands of what looked like the gingiva in a mouth. His dad had been a dentist, and this looked like pulpy flesh.

I'm in a goddamned throat. Wonder if the rest of them feel it?

He wanted to look around, but didn't indulge the paranoid desire. *Something might leap out at him from the front. Why worry about the people behind him?*

Twenty feet in, the rough-hewn passage leveled out. *The floor is smooth, at least.*

He could see a faint light through a doorway about fifty feet further in.

Paused a moment, and looked back, taking a head count. Marks was right behind, followed by Jackson, then the medic, Botts, and Tircek, the geologist.

Where was Sola?

"Sola is missing. Anybody see anything?"

The headlamps made faceplates completely transparent. He saw a gamut of emotions, but none apparently were feeling the panic coursing through him: Except Jackson. *He's as spooked as I am.*

He watched Jackson key his circuit for Sola, but couldn't hear anything. "Looks like we have some interference down here. No indirect communications. Not even with the shuttle or Cormorant."

Marks pushed past Botts, heading back toward the entrance. "Bet she found some plant back there and doesn't even know we're gone."

"Now wait a minute," said Jackson. "We can't afford to split up."

"Well then, sir, why did we take any non-military types with us then? You know the way they are," said Marks.

"You're bordering on insubordination, Sergeant! We didn't know what we'd run into down here."

"What do you suggest we do, sir? Do we wait for her to catch up?"

Crane wondered if maybe Sergeant Marks was a little edgier than he thought. *I'm definitely not enjoying this, and Jackson normally keeps it together pretty well, but not this time. Doesn't look like he has a clue what to do.*

"We will all go," said Jackson.

"There is a light ahead, Commander," said Tircek. "I'd like to check it out. It might be the source of the transmission."

"By yourself?"

"Sola will understand. Besides, my one gun wouldn't make much difference, would it?"

Jackson hesitated a moment longer, then said, "Crane, stay with him."

Crane watched as the others turned to head back the way they had come in search of Sola. *Thanks a lot. Goddamn Sola. All that mattered to her was research. Now, I'm stuck down here with a giant freak.*

"Shall we proceed, Private Crane?" Tircek asked.

He sighed, "Yeah, Doc, let's get this over with."

Chapter 4

SOLA

Sola's stubbornness paid dividends. It was so easy to slip behind everyone. Tircek grinned at her, but said nothing. She liked him, but he was hard to know. He kept to himself and refused to discuss his past. He'd talk all day about humanity's past, linguistics, or rocks, but nothing personal. *Probably best to maintain distance, anyway. Relationships equaled entanglements.*

Nothing illustrated that better than her break-up with Dr. Norman Botts two days ago. He hadn't accepted their friendship well. *Anyway, none of that mattered. She needed to get away from the overprotective gaze of Jackson and the two soldiers.*

The moment Tircek turned his attention away, she slipped back up the passage. *Odds were good that they wouldn't even miss her. Still, every moment counted. You only got one chance with Jackson.*

Back at the entrance, she settled the All-One carefully against her right hip, and moved the strap to her left shoulder. Now she could brace it with her right and carry her pistol in her left hand.

She turned left, back onto the crumbling stone path, feeling her pulse speed up. More of the birds were at the top of the temple above her, but she had enough footage for now. She wanted a closer look at some two- and three-story buildings a block further east.

A terrible odor enveloped her as she reached the first of the buildings a block away. A series of symbols decorated the wall beside what appeared to be a door. No handles or buttons. The entire stone building glittered with mica. *Granite? Not my specialty.*

She stepped closer, still recording, but now also scanning the rock. Details of the building's composition scrolled across her screen. Something about Muscovite Shist. *This was an important find! My insubordination is going to pay off!*

Data continued to spew across the screen. She took one more step and a cool breeze washed over her. Startled, she looked up. The door was open, but it was too dark inside to see anything. The stench strengthened, wafting from somewhere within.

She switched her All-One light on and played the beam across the opening. Something huge snarled and came straight for her. Dying afternoon sunlight played over a scaled hide while the thing bared its fangs and took a swipe at her with a claw. The razor-sharp talons cut right through her wrist that controlled the All-One. The piece of flesh and machinery flew free.

Sola staggered, blood spouting from the ragged stump of her right hand. Too shocked to scream or even react, her back slammed against the wall behind her. The thing followed her out and scooped her up into its arms. Her vision faded in and out. She focused long enough to see her hand clutching the pistol in her lap, just as the thing carried her through the doorway.

Chapter 5

JACKSON

Jackson followed, taking the rear-guard spot. Paranoia and a strong desire to see Leila again gave him all the motivation he needed. Just seeing the sun was comforting as they emerged back outside.

"Anyone see Sola?" he asked.

"She's vanished, sir," Marks answered.

Jackson looked for the shuttle. All he could see were ruins. He keyed his connection to the shuttle. "You still with us, Tran?"

"I'm here, Commander. Something wrong?"

"Not sure. Sola's missing. Keep an eye out for her, please."

"Yes, sir," Tran replied.

"She's way over the line on this one. Doesn't listen!" Marks said.

Out of the corner of his eye, Jackson noticed the hunched figure of Botts climbing the steps, or whatever they were, of the temple above them. He couldn't tell if they resembled Aztec, Mayan, or even Toltec ruins, but they looked like the picture in his mind of them.

The top of the temple was a hundred feet up, but Botts kept climbing. Apparently, he wouldn't be any better at taking orders than Sola.

"Where are you going, Botts?" Jackson asked.

"The view is better from up here, sir. Is that ok?"

"Ask next time."

Botts didn't even turn around.

"Botts, watch out for the birds!" Marks yelled.

"I see them, Sergeant. My assault rifle is an excellent fowling piece."

Someone knows we're here. That thought kept turning over in Jackson's mind. *Something lowered the planetary shields. The nature of it, dead, living, or robotic, didn't matter, just the intent. With Sola missing, everything takes on sinister connotations.* Jackson noticed that something had cracked or buckled the stone flagstones of the street. Few buildings looked intact. There were no skyscrapers like in a human city, and certainly nothing taller than this temple-type structure.

A block down, a black object on the ground caught his attention.

"Marks, Botts, I think I see something."

Chapter 6

CRANE

Tircek lowered his head to clear the doorway and entered, shotgun in hand. He stopped a few feet in. Over his shoulder, he said, "You smoke, Private?"

"Not really, Doc, but why do you ask?" Crane answered, stopping beside the scientist. What he saw in the room clenched his stomach, left him pasty-faced and nauseous.

"I vote to take off these damn hoods and have a smoke."

From somewhere far away, Crane heard himself answer, "Commander Jackson won't like that."

Tircek raised an eyebrow at him. "Lotta things the commander doesn't like. Readings check out on my All-One. I can make some decisions for myself. Join me." With that, the giant reached up and unfastened the seals around his neck and pulled the whole hood and helmet pieces off. His close-cropped blond hair looked sweaty and his pale face was flushed. "There, that's much better."

While the man fished around in a pouch fastened to his waist belt, Crane undid the seals on his mask and helmet. The air felt great on his skin. He could feel it drying the sweat almost immediately. Thank God there was no smell.

Didn't wear it long enough to stink yet.

Tircek used a small tool to cut off the end of a cigar, then handed it to him.

The room held machinery, human furniture, and shredded mummified cadavers. *A last stand, maybe?* Mixed in with the human remains were inch-long metallic flakes or scales.

"Light?" Tircek asked, with a lighter in hand. Crane leaned over, watched the flame, took a puff or two and then straightened up. Tircek put the lighter in the pouch on his waist.

"Pleasant aroma," Crane remarked.

"I took the best I could get, some Cuban parejos, before we left. Save them for special occasions."

"You calling this a special occasion?"

Tircek inclined his head back and blew a perfect smoke ring. "I don't believe in parallel evolution, Private."

"You're suggesting that those are human corpses?"

Tircek nodded.

Crane took a tentative puff. "I'm glad you get paid to think about it. All I know is I want out. After being on the ship for so long, being outside is great."

Tircek walked over toward the banks of machines and Crane trailed along behind him. *Something was active here.* The big man lowered himself carefully into a chair before a console. He reached over his shoulder and pulled his All-One from a sheath built into his backpack. He then inserted an earbud in his right ear. "The All-One is connecting. This is the source of the signal, or transmission," he said, patting the console in front of him. "The language isn't one we know."

"I hear nothing," said Crane, settling into a chair beside him.

"No, you wouldn't. The broadcast channel is higher than you can hear. I hope the All-One can make something of it. It is the same message over and over."

"You can hear it, with that earplug or whatever it is?"

"I hear something, but I'm not sure what it is yet. Here, put my extra plug in your ear and hear for yourself."

Crane took the earphone. For a moment, there was nothing. Then a sharp pain spiked through his head, static, distorted images flickering by a voice speaking. Not just sound... The man had a lined, tired face. He spoke, but the picture faded out. *"The home worlds are all dead. Our enemy has defeated us, but we have chased them across four solar systems. They fight to the last."*

More static...

"... and just like that, all Hell broke loose in the jungle. All around us the vegetation parted and creatures straight out of nightmare charged. Our enemy, the Aztarz, was bipedal and humanoid in form, but that was all they had in common with humanity. Each of them had four arms extending from their torsos, and their skin scaled, not flesh. Large, forked tongues dangled from their mouths as they hissed with fury at us. I gave the order: 'Fire! Take them down!' I screamed at the top of my lungs, yanking my weapon from the holster on my hip. Our group's fire tore into the lizard-like savages with little effect. A few of them crumpled to the ground, but most kept coming despite the large holes blown in their bodies. 'By all the Hells of Kreor!' I yelled as I placed a dozen rounds in the lead creature and watched it keep coming without so much as flinching. It leaped onto me, tearing at my armor with four sets of razor like talons and a mouthful of gleaming, metallic teeth. I screamed as the beast ripped my cuirass apart. I felt its filthy talons rake across my ribs as my blood sprayed onto the alien soil below the Aztarz's feet. Not far away, my friend Ulan lay dead while the creatures tore chunks of his flesh from his body and chewed with a series of sickening, smacking sounds.

I pressed the muzzle of my gun against its head and pulled the trigger.

Lady Calyn and my brother Ellec carried me beneath a temple not far into the city. We made our last stand... "

"Wake up, Crane! Wake up!"

Chapter 7

JACKSON

Jackson checked to make sure his weapon was ready, then started a slow jog toward the distant object. Marks followed along on the other side of the street by a few steps.

"Aren't we waiting for Botts, sir?" asked Marks.

"Nope! Dumbass should be listening to orders. Tired of people ignoring me." He stumbled a bit on a loose piece of masonry. His breath came a little heavy. He needed to spend more time in the gym.

They ran past the rubble of two more houses and slowed to a walk.

An All-One lay on the street, just past the still intact wall of a house. Sola's hand still held onto the machine. *Where was the rest of her? Hidden around the corner?*

"Sola?" whispered Jackson, his breathing growing strained.

No one answered.

Marks started forward.

"No, let me, Sergeant. She was my responsibility."

Behind them, the sound of Botts' labored breathing and clattering boots drew closer.

Jackson edged up, then spun around the corner, submachine gun held braced against his hip.

Sola wasn't there. Her blood stood out against the bleached white stone. *We have made a sacrifice.*

Marks and Botts rounded the corner together.

"Time to get out of here," Jackson said. "We'll get Tircek and Crane and then get the hell out of here."

"I'll second that," said Botts.

Chapter 8

CRANE

"We have what we need, Crane! Wake up!"

The voice got through. Crane realized he'd been ignoring it.

"Ok, Doc, I'm back with you. I was living some guy's last moments there."

"Unless you want to repeat that experience, we need to leave now, Private!"

Crane scrambled to his feet, grabbing his weapon on the way up. Tircek was already turning away from him, heading for the doorway.

A bestial snarl outside in the passage caused both men to stop. Tircek lifted his shotgun, fitting the folding stock against his shoulder. *Thank God he's with me and not Botts.*

An awful smell of rot swept into the room. Standing framed in the doorway was a monster. The head was bulbous on top, with a single eye on a segmented stalk set just above a maw of serrated teeth. The eye retreated under a heavy brow as the thing stepped closer. There were four arms, each ending with three finger talons, a barrel-chested torso, and two legs.

Crane panicked. The submachine gun jerked in his hands as he squeezed the trigger. The extended burst climbed from the bottom of the creature's torso right to the top of its skull and into the ceiling, the bullets parting scales and flesh like putty.

He fired until the magazine ran dry. His ears rang from the weapon's roar.

"Calm down, Private. Better re-load before we go any further."

Crane heard himself whimper. "Ain't killed nothing before, Doc. Couldn't help it."

"Better get a grip, soon son. Panic will kill us for sure."

The bigger man stepped past Crane, and over the corpse, while Crane re-loaded.

He slipped the empty magazine into a cargo pocket on his pants and pulled a fresh one from the ammo pouch on his belt, and slotted it up into the well. *Fresh fifty rounds. I better not waste this one. Wonder why this guy isn't afraid? Since when do scientists have nerves of steel?*

"Sure you don't want me to go first, Doctor?" he asked.

The doctor turned around. "Hell yes, you go first. I don't need an itchy trigger finger behind me!"

Ouch!

"Guess I deserved that. I feel better now. The shakes are gone."

"Ok, then do your thing, Private, and I'll cover the retreat."

Crane pushed past and hurried up the passage, back toward the light and open sky.

Chapter 9

JACKSON

They all ran.

"You should have grabbed Sola's All-One, I said!" said Botts. Even through the visor, his face was red, and his hair stringy from sweat. The flush on each of his cheeks looked unhealthy. He wasn't in good shape. Too much time in a starship.

"There was no time," snapped Marks.

"Her death is for nothing without her research. Isn't that worth anything to you, Commander?"

Jackson shrugged. "Chance, we all take, Doctor."

"She might not even be dead. With her All-One, we would know."

"She's dead..." said Marks.

The hunchbacked man glared at the soldier. *Other than his rounded back, he was normal, even good-looking. No weakling either. The guy's got a pair of arms and shoulders on him.*

"I'm going back for it, by myself if I have to," Botts said.

Marks snorted and looked over at Jackson. "You going to let this egghead dictate to us, sir?"

Jackson thought about it. *The scientist had a point. Everything was for nothing if they returned to Cormorant with no records.*

"Ok, Doctor, we get the All-One, and then you do what you're told until we go back to the ship."

Botts might have grinned, but Jackson couldn't be sure. The other man was already running back the way they came.

Jackson and Marks followed, but not with much enthusiasm. Both of them slowed to a walk as Botts increased the distance between them. The civilian was over a block ahead when he reached Sola's All-One and grabbed it. He picked up her hand and put it into a sample bag. He then jogged back to them.

"These people got no instinct for self-preservation, sir. Sooner we're off this rock, the happier I'll be."

"Guess that single-mindedness comes in handy when they need to focus, Sergeant, but it sucks to look out for them."

Marks grinned.

In the sergeant's eyes, Jackson was just a Communication Officer. The stories still floated around the ship about when Jackson was the Recruiting Officer for the 2nd Fleet on Tiberius Twelve, otherwise known as Tiberius Brown's Planet. They all knew he had balls and having the respect of soldiers was important to him.

"You know, sir, for a borderline civilian, you aren't a bad guy."

"We get grunt training, Marks. If we had to, I could call down an orbital barrage. Can you say the same?"

Marks shook his head. "That's part of the training I'll get at the Advanced NCO school on Bacchus Two."

"That one of those hell planets that barely supports life?"

"It ain't a vacation hotspot."

Just then, Botts caught up to them, and all three ran toward the temple.

"Can't believe you picked up her hand," said Marks.

"There will be evidence of what severed her hand. Being thorough is vital to accuracy."

"You soulless fuck!"

Marks trailed off as Tircek and Crane backed out of the temple, guns blazing.

"Hurry," Jackson said, taking a ragged breath.

Something followed Tircek up and out of the passage, despite two blasts from his shotgun. Crane tripped and sprawled on the ground behind Tircek. The bigger man trampled him in his haste to get out of the range of the rampaging creature following them.

Talons ripped across Tircek's left thigh and he fell, finger pressing down on the trigger of his weapon. Five or six shots from the shotgun ripped the four-armed, scaly thing apart. A good portion of its torso vanished along with the top of its head. The remains splattered over Crane.

Crane stood up, with violet ichor spattered all over his back. Tircek fired once more and needed to re-load. Two more of the creatures sprang from the tunnel and grabbed Crane. Tircek stumbled backwards as Crane fell face first.

"Fall back!" Marks ordered. "Head for the shuttle!"

"Negative on that!" Jackson said over the comm link in his helmet. "They have us cut-off. Follow me!"

To his credit, Tircek didn't abandon Crane. The big man tossed the empty shotgun aside and waded into the creatures, striking out with his ham-sized fists. At his feet, Crane writhed in agony as the two creatures tore him apart. His left arm and leg were already severed, and Jackson glimpsed his haggard face just as one creature snapped its jaws closed. A primed grenade popped free from Crane's right hand and rolled two inches.

"Tircek run!" shouted Botts, seeing the same thing Jackson did.

Tircek ignored him and instead grabbed the head of the second creature and shoved his fingers into its eye.

The grenade went off. Most of Crane and his killer vanished, while Tircek and his adversary caught the rest of the blast. Both of them flew a short distance and landed without grace in a boneless sprawl.

More creatures poured out of the tunnel.

Jackson panicked. *What are we doing just standing here watching our shipmates die?* He forced himself into action. "They're coming for us! On the double, let's go!"

Roars and enraged snarls followed them as they ran through the ruins. Jackson tried to focus on the map scrolling across the interior of his visor. "Tran, can you hear me?"

"Yes sir! I've been monitoring all channels. Ready to be picked up?"

"Yes! Can you see the location on my visor map board?"

"Looks like a small hill inside the jungle."

"That's right! We are close to the city's fringe now. I estimate we will be at that location in less than two minutes."

"I'll be there, sir!"

"Good. Jackson out!"

"Tran out."

Jackson jumped a low wall and felt the spring of coiled grass under his boots. He sprinted through the jungle, firing at the monsters that followed.

Botts and Marks were behind him as the shuttle streaked through the sky above. The whine of its engine was deafening even inside his suit as Jackson took stock of the situation. Half of his team was missing, taken by the lizard things. Marks was hopping aboard the shuttle, which had hit the ground with its bay door already open. Botts raced past and threw himself inside the ship. Jackson stopped, bracing himself in the doorway. One more look around and he spotted Tircek limping after them. He had his gun and Crane's. How did he get away? Maybe the things had had enough?

The creatures seemed to stand off.

A moment or two later, Jackson helped Tircek swing aboard and then he closed the hatch. As soon as he did, the shuttle lifted off at full power. It shot upwards into the sky, back towards the *Cormorant* in orbit. All of them crowded together on two benches.

Too many lost for nothing, Jackson thought. *Even two is too many.*

"Did you see those things?" Tircek asked. "They were rotting."

"What?" Jackson asked. All he'd noticed was that monsters were alien and lizard-like.

"Their scales... their wounds," Tircek informed him. "We didn't do all that damage. They were dead already when they came at us."

"You're crazy, man," Marks said.

"Our bullets didn't even faze them," Tircek continued. "It was as if they couldn't feel a thing we did to them. Even when we shot their limbs clean off, they just kept coming."

Marks stared at Tircek. "Uh, doctor... Your bio-suit has tears in it."

Tircek sighed, looking down at his wounded thigh, and several cuts on his arms. "No worries, Sergeant. I'm sure our decon protocols will catch anything that might be a danger. I was lucky that alien absorbed the worst of the grenade for me, although I am almost deaf now."

Jackson thought of the lizard things below and shuddered. "I hope so, Doctor," he said. "I hope so." *At least their mission was supposed to be over soon, and they'd head home. That might change now. Which way would the captain go with this? He was ready to be done. They'd been stuck together, out here in space, far too long.*

All except him and Leila. She could replace a few terrible moments in his mind. Yes, indeed.

Chapter 10

2122 A.D.   PETER

*P*eter kicked off the floor, floating up the work shaft towards the Hyperion's engine room. The repairs had gone smoothly. After five years in deep space, the ship was holding up remarkably well. He smiled as he neared the top of the shaft and reached out, taking hold of the access ladder. He positioned himself on it and said, "Gravity on." Climbing the last few feet, he pulled himself up into the engine room. Claudia was waiting for him.

"Do you have to do that?" she asked. Her grin always stopped his heart for a beat or two.

Peter laughed. "What's the point of being in space if we don't fly from time to time?"

"You're standing a little close, aren't you, mister?" A lock of her long blond hair fell over her left eye as she looked up at him.

"Not close enough," he said, reaching out and pulling her close. He leaned down for a kiss. Their lips met briefly, and he ran a hand down her back. She pulled away, putting distance between them.

This time she's still smiling. Am I forgiven?

"The captain wants to see you," she informed him. "He wants to know if everything is ready for the leap home."

Peter shook his head. "Earth. I still can't believe we're headed back already. Where did the years go?"

"You aren't ready to go back?"

"Not sure. Thank god the mission was a success."

Her smile faltered. "Will you let your grudge against the captain go? Things may not be so rosy for you soon. Why chance throwing twelve years away? You could end up an engineer's mate on a tramp ship to a convict planet."

"Probably more what I'm suited for. You know I'll never see eye to eye with him. God knows I never expected to be a Fletcher Christian on the goddamned Bounty, and I can never forgive myself for siding with him."

"I'm sorry, Peter..."

Reach out. Now! Here's your chance.

He ignored the voice. "What gets me, Claudia, is that he never realized how the whole crew felt. I'll go see what he wants."

Might have been my last chance.

Chapter 11

EDWARDS

C aptain Edwards looked up from the logs he was going through as Peter entered his workroom.

"Heard you wanted to see me?"

Edwards scowled at the engineer. Five years aboard one of the most advanced ships in the fleet, under his own tight rein, hadn't diminished the man's casual attitude in the slightest. "Take a seat, Hoyle," Edwards gestured across his desk towards the chair opposite from him. Peter plopped into it.

"Is she ready for the leap?"

"All systems are go. She just needs another half hour to finish powering up."

"Good," Edwards nodded.

The *Hyperion* was massive, built to explore beyond the borders of known space. She was a cross between a science vessel and a heavy warship. Shaped like a strange-looking cruise missile, she was eight-hundred-fifty meters long and contained many decks and a fighter/shuttle bay. Most of her space was empty and the large stockpiles of supplies depleted from her long voyage. Her hull had many sensor modules and communications arrays, but they were gone. The gray metal of her exterior armor showed the trauma she'd suffered a year before from emerging too close to a young star. By a miracle, she'd built power and leaped away again before her nine monster-sized space engines burned out and the gravity well pulled her into the giant fusion reactor. Still, she had suffered a lot of damage. They brought the primary systems back online and her leap drive was functional enough to keep her moving and get her home. She was presently back inside known space and within a single quick leap of Earth.

Edwards hated being out of touch with Earth Command. He presumed they'd long ago written off the *Hyperion* as lost. He and his crew had received their last communique from Earth Command over a year and a half ago and it was time-delayed by the lag of traveling through actual space. No one had invented a means of sending signals through the void of leap space yet. That kind of instantaneous, real-time communication still belonged to the realm of science fiction if the parties were more than an AU apart. They were in range, but with no equipment to send or receive a message. Command was going to be in for a quite a shock when they dropped out of leap space into Earth orbit.

The short range comm, gear of the shuttles, and fighters still worked, so Edwards planned to launch a shuttle and establish a channel to Earth Command before it took them as hostile and open fired. It was risky, but it was his only option. Besides, Earth's sensors should instantly recognize the *Hyperion* as she appeared, but Edwards always liked to prepare for the worst-case scenario. The other forty-nine members of his crew had learned to be thankful for his cautiousness during their long trip. His grim zeal had saved the ship more than once.

"Forget one more time to address me properly, Hoyle. Just once more."

"Sorry about that, sir."

"You presume too much. I want you on the shuttle and pick four good people to go with you."

31

"How about Claudia Coyne, Garrett Fergusson, Janet Donner, and Frank Litz?"

"Good. Let me know the minute the drive's charged."

Peter and turned his attention back to reviewing the ship's logs, so they'd be ready for his debriefing upon their arrival.

Chapter 12

PETER

Can't get past this bad feeling. Why dread going home? Peter wondered.

The seconds ticked by until the initial vibration of the drive engaged. It was a feeling he'd never get used to: the sudden gut-wrenching sensation of falling forwards; the sound of an angel chorus droning up and down the scale. The leaps seemed to last forever. Outside the *Hyperion*, the stars disappeared and the whole of existence filled with the blood red nothingness of Leap space. Then, the mighty ship dropped back into reality above the Earth. Moments later, the shield serving as the shuttle bay door flickered out, and Peter leaned back in the pilot chair. He spoke into his helmet microphone: "This is shuttle Alpha 2-9. We're leaving the bay now. All systems go." He glanced at Claudia beside him. Her eyes were already closed.

Edwards didn't reply.

As the engines of the *Hyperion's* leap drive powered down, and with only a slight hesitation, Peter fired the shuttle's thrusters, quickly gained lift and speed, and exited the shuttle bay. *Hyperion's* bulk was to their left, and there, glittering below them, was an orb of vibrant blues and greens shining beautifully in the blackness surrounding it. Earth. Home.

Claudia's voice beside him: "*Hyperion* Shuttle Two-Nine to Earth Command, over?"

No one answered.

"Luna Central, do you read me? Orbital Command?" Peter listened to her try these and other separate stations without response.

The door behind them, to the passenger cabin, opened. Garrett poked his head in. "We having problems?"

Peter said, over his shoulder, "No response from any station."

"Peter," Claudia said, her voice filled with urgency. Peter spun around in his seat. "What is it?"

"I've got four fighters inbound on an intercept course."

Peter took a glance at the sensor data himself. "What the...?"

The shuttle's database couldn't identify the make of the fighters. They had the same sleek manta shape of the Hades Class, but appeared to be reconfigured. Their engines were burning hot, as if their radiation scrubbers were off line.

This made little sense. If Earth Command truly saw the *Hyperion* as hostile or a threat, they'd be dust by now. So why did the fighters all have their weapons locked on them?

"I'm getting a message," Claudia said. She punched a few keys on her station's console and a hollow, gravelly voice filled the pilot's compartment. "Welcome home, crew of the *Hyperion*. I wish we could say we'd been expecting you. Please recall your shuttle. We'll board shortly. A decon vessel is already in route to your position."

"This is *Hyperion* shuttle Alpha 2-9. The Hyperion has taken damage. She has no communication capabilities."

No reply came. Garrett leaned into the front of the shuttle, looking at Peter and Claudia. "Don't regulations require that we report to the nearest space dock for decon and debriefing?"

Peter glared at Garrett, knowing the man was right. "Earth Command, did you say a decon ship is in route to us?"

"Much has changed in your time away, Alpha 2-9. We board all ships for inspection and preliminary decontamination before being allowed to dock with any orbital facility. I understand your communication problems. Please return to the *Hyperion* and prepare to be boarded."

"Yes, sir," Peter answered curtly.

"Well, that's certainly weird," Garrett commented.

Most of the *Hyperion's* crew gathered in the spacious hangar outside the docking/launching area of the ship's shuttle bay. Peter's news of the Hyperion being boarded traveled fast. Everyone not at a crucial post wanted to be there to meet their guests. They were eager to know what happened on Earth. Captain Edwards, Peter, and Garrett stood at the front of the crowd.

Peter glanced toward Claudia, where she stood in the last rank of crewmen in front of the entrance to the Ready Room. She smiled. Peter's bad feeling lingered. Garrett was the ranking officer of the small contingent of marines stationed on the ship and wore a sidearm on his hip. He was the only armed crew member present.

The docking area airlock dilated open and the first Decon party member stepped into the hangar. The crew applauded and cheered. Their presence meant they'd made it. They were home at last. The Decon officer wore a full body bio-suit and jet-black armor covering him from head to toe. The suit's sleek faceplate concealed his face. He carried a kit bag in his right hand. Six more Decon squad members followed him. They carried combat shotguns with expanded magazines.

Captain Edwards stepped forward to meet the officer with the kit. "What's the meaning of this? Why are you armed?"

"Calm yourself," the officer said, holding a hand out towards the captain, warning him to stay back. "The Earth is at war. We inspect ships for alien pathogens and other threats to the security of the planet. If you resist, I have the authority to order have you shot."

Edwards went white at the officer's threat. The entire hangar fell silent, their attention fixated on the confrontation between Edwards and the Decon officer. Peter felt Garrett give him a nudge. The Decon squad spread out, flanking the crowd, as if they were finding better firing positions. This can't be happening. There has to be an explanation. Garrett leaned in close. "Be ready," he whispered. Peter shot him a glance back, wondering what he was supposed to be ready for.

Edwards stood frozen, and Peter wondered how the Decon process was going to be carried out, when the Decon officer barked, "Take them!"

All six of the armed squad members opened up at once. Their weapons thundered again and again as they dropped one target and moved on to the next. Peter watched the captain go down, a large needle like projectile sticking out from his chest. The hangar erupted into a panicked chaos of screams and gunshots.

He looked for Garrett, but the marine leader was already on the floor. His gun lay a few feet from his hand.

Peter jumped for the weapon and snatched it up. Half of the gathered crew was already down. No sign of Claudia, though. He ducked into the panicked mass, desperate to reach the Ready Room.

Nothing he could do would help the others. One man with a single pistol couldn't make a stand against seven armed people in bio-armor. He hoped to warn survivors, and find Claudia. If God was with them, they could deal with the boarding party and get the Hyperion the hell out of here. He didn't know how many of the crew stayed at their posts, but he guessed it to be at least a dozen.

Frank was probably on the bridge. He and Claudia weren't much higher on Edward's list than he was.

People cried out and fell all around him: White uniformed figures, smeared crimson, some friends, all of them familiar, falling, screaming. Suddenly, living was going to be a tall order.

The crowd thinned out as he stumbled through the Ready Room door. Three bodies sprawled near the row of benches and the long line of lockers: Two men, and the third a blonde-haired woman with a needle in her back.

"Claudia!" he screamed.

A hand grabbed his shoulder, and he spun, unaware of the hate contorting his face, and the snarl that issued from his lips. One of the Decon soldiers! Without hesitation, he pressed the pistol up against the man's faceplate and fired. Liquified bone and brain splattered across Peter's face, chest, and arms. The horrible stench of putrefied flesh filled his nose, cloying and overpowering.

The corpse sagged backwards, and he helped it along with a shove.

He shared the room with the dead.

Claudia must be alive!

He felt for a pulse in her neck. As his fingers touched her skin, she moaned. Thank God!

"Hang in there, babe, just hold on. I'm with you." He lifted her without removing the needle. Better to leave it there for now. He ran, the pistol in his right hand as he cradled her in his arms. Blood ran from the edge of her mouth. So much blood. Red emergency lighting strobed as he stepped into the passage and turned left. The alarm sirens drowned out the sound of his sobbing breath and pounding boots.

Got to reach the escape pod! The onboard robodoc will save her!

Chapter 13

FRANK

He sat paralyzed in the command chair, listening to the screams, the gunfire, and then a brief interval of silence. Each time a new situation confronted him, he hesitated, but the delay had shortened since the beginning of the voyage. Of course, most people thought he was just slow. Poor Frank, befuddled again.

Nothing could be farther than the truth. He looked up at the three screens across the room from him. The third from the left was what they called the tactical view. The symbols for the immense bulk of a heavy cruiser and an escort carrier were now present, roughly forty miles from *Hyperion*. A cloud of lesser ships, probably more fighters and perhaps shuttles, were halfway to the *Hyperion*. The names of the two ships appeared above the symbols: The heavy cruiser was the *Julio Cesare* and the escort carrier was the *Roma*.

That's strange. Both ships were being decommissioned years ago. Doesn't look good.

Most of *Hyperion's* weapons systems could operate independently of human control, but it identified all the current targets as friendly. *Have to change the targeting parameters now!* The menu was beneath his fingertips. *But almost everyone is dead!*

The middle screen on the wall showed the ship's interior, over-head, deck by deck. A flick of his finger cycled through each one. All surviving personnel identified and highlighted in green, and hostiles outlined in red.

The hostiles out-numbered the survivors.

Not going to win the battle within or without. Need to gather anybody I can and get the hell off ship!

Frank paused a last time. Three survivors were making for the escape pod on Deck Three. At least, that was what he surmised. Nothing else was there. One last look at the screens and a quick stop by the drop shaft door at the arms locker. Nothing heavy like a rifle in there, unfortunately, but there were two specialized shotgun pistols, both equipped with 10 round drum magazines. He took the pistols and a handful of loaded magazines.

With a pistol in either hand, he stopped by the door, waited for it to slide open, then stepped out into the shaft. "Gravity on," he said, and fell like a stone in a deep well.

A moment or two later he said, "Gravity off," and felt the abrupt shift drag him to an immediate halt, almost exactly even with the ladder rungs and the door to Deck Three.

Such a fall may have injured a human, but Frank's body could withstand far greater impacts. He reached out, guns still drawn, and hooked his hands through the rungs, pulling himself toward the door. The panel slid to the side into the wall, and he exited onto the key passage that ran the length of the ship.

Frank almost ran into the backs of two Decon Soldiers. As it was, they were turning toward him as he ran toward them, firing both pistols, point blank. One soldier took two shots, one to the chest and another to the neck. The second took two shots to the groin and collapsed against the wall. At near point-blank range, the heavy solid slugs tore them both to pieces, leaving huge gaping wounds despite their armor. Frank plunged past them, but continued to fire as the two men refuse to stay down! Two shots from a Laymon Hand Cannon were *usually* more than enough to put down an elephant.

The guy with the groin shot on the right swung his rifle around. Frank fired twice more, and the man's head disintegrated in a welter of blood, bone, and maggots. A terrible rotten egg stench filled the air, and Frank spun on his heels toward the other man. He fired twice more with the left-hand gun, aware only of an explosion of foul black gore and ivory white bone.

He kept running, jumping over the humanoid-shaped remains of a security bot.

Almost there! The next right...

More soldiers! Where'd they come from?

Worst of all, right in front of the pod's entrance lay the bodies of Peter and Claudia. And then there were three soldiers with slug-firing rifles centered on his chest.

The soldier on the left sneered and said, "Drop the guns and live. We will spare the lives of these others if you do."

Frank dropped the guns.

"Now, empty your pockets!"

Frank dropped the extra magazines of ammo beside the guns. The soldier motioned him to step back, then reached down and picked everything up.

Soldiers lifted Peter and Claudia's bodies and escorted Frank to the hangar bay. There were now five shuttles docked aboard the Hyperion. Frank watched as they loaded his friends like meat into a ship.

"Human, you do not know how lucky you are. We need some prisoners. If it wasn't for what you and your friends know about this ship and its mission, I would frag you right now. Get onto the shuttle. You'll be flying up front with me where I can keep an eye you on. Place the woman in the robodoc."

Why is he calling me Human, and what's with the rotten smell and putrid flesh when I shot them? He'd ask those questions later, when he could force an answer out of them.

The shuttle door closed. The temperature was far colder than most humans preferred it. He noticed none of the Decon squad removed their armor.

Frank took a seat in the large pilot's area with the commander, the pilot, and two armed guards. Peter was still back watching over Claudia while she was in the robodoc. One guard stood watch. The shuttle's engines roared to life, and the craft left the *Hyperion* for the blackness of space. "This is cargo Shuttle 3 requesting permission to enter Earth's atmosphere with prisoners on board."

"Permission granted, Shuttle 3. What is your destination?"

"We're in route to New York, the science center of Dr. Gallows. ETA fifteen minutes."

"Understood, Shuttle 3."

Frank watched the fiery rage of Earth's atmosphere burning over the shuttle's forward window as it dove downwards. It broke through the clouds into open air, with the city of New York far below. Frank peered out, watching every detail emerge as they drew closer. New York had changed. Gone were the glittering towers of humanity and the bright lights. Instead, the city sprawling out was largely in ruins, and missing many familiar landmarks. Now, dark spear-like towers rose to touch the gray clouds of the sky. Great swathes of the original city appeared to be underwater. The shuttle landed on a platform of one of the few remaining original buildings and Frank disembarked with his guards leading the way.

I wonder if the sky is always gray now?

The guard who took his pistols removed his helmet. He was a hulking man with peeling skin. He kicked Peter and Claudia. "Get up, up or we will turn you over to the Beasts!"

Peter scrambled to his feet and helped Claudia up. Her face was gray, but she stood with Peter's arm around her. The guards herded them out of the ship.

"Beasts?" Peter asked.

"You'll find out on your own," said another guard.

On a nearby platform, a second shuttle disgorged its passengers.

"That's our crew," said Claudia.

"But how, I see the Captain and Fergusson? Aren't they dead? I'm sure they were." said Peter.

"You'll find out soon enough," the hulking guard growled.

Not long after, the guards herded them through an Iris door and down a series of dimly lit passages. They passed several featureless doors. Without warning, or any instructions, the guards stopped at a door that looked like all the others.

"Open up 48 Jimmy," said the hulking guard to the smaller man beside him.

"Sure thing, Vic." The smaller guard pointed something in his hand at a nearby door marked with the numerals 48, and the door opened. Vic pushed them all inside. "Relax while you can, meat," he said. "The end is near!"

"Meat?" asked Peter.

"That's what he said," said Claudia.

The room was small, with three bunks and a toilet.

Frank stood in front of them both. "I'll get you both out of here, if I can. It just may be tricky."

"Listen, Frank," said Claudia, "I'm so sorry about the incident in the Virtual World, but..."

"Don't trouble yourself, Claudia. It doesn't matter. It never did."

He watched her eyes, then her mouth on that one.

"What do you mean? I know I hurt you. That Peter hurt you."

"I was confused and hurt until I understood. After that, it didn't matter."

43

Both Peter and Claudia stared at him. "That is a healthy attitude there," said Peter. "Gotta admit you surprise me constantly. Thought you were a dullard."

Frank grinned at him. "Funny, I always thought the same about you."

Claudia laughed. "He won that round, Peter."

"Guess so."

Frank raised his hand. "You both look tired. Why don't both of you try to get some rest while I stand guard?"

"You mean that, Frank?" said Claudia.

"Yes, go ahead."

She looked tired. Within moments, he could tell they were both asleep.

Chapter 14

CLAUDIA

She fell, a headlong plunge, down into sleep, into a memory. Her wounds were only healed halfway, and she was so tired...

The wind blew restlessly in the trees. She lost herself in the sweet grinding, rocking motion where their bodies met and merged. So close... so close.

She heard, felt a distant concussive boom, and both of them looked up. In that instant, a wave of unreality washed over her and she could feel her body floating in womb-like darkness. The sun dimmed and complete confusion settled in. *Where am I?* Then the light returned.

The man's handsome face was beneath her and their fingers interlocked, where she held him down against the earth. His eyes were a brilliant blue. The sweet dying sensation built, and he whispered her name as they found release and their limbs convulsed.

"Claudia!" an anguished voice shouted in the distance.

"Sounds like the cripple," he said.

Her anger rose right to the surface. "Don't call him that!"

"You want me to lie?"

"I want you to have some compassion."

45

"Goddamn it, Claudia, he is my friend too, but he is what he is. He takes twice as long to learn anything. I'd call that mentally crippled."

She shook her head and levered herself up and away from him. He had an exasperated look on his face and his blue eyes were cold. Wintery. *Why didn't I ever notice that before?* "You are a bastard, Peter."

He gave her that lazy grin, full of mockery.

"Claudia!" The voice was closer, and there was nowhere to hide. Aside from the sleeping bag they were lying on, just leaves were underfoot, and the rotted remains of several fallen trees.

Where are my clothes? She looked around, taking a step or two toward the nearby stream. *Ah, there! Right next to the stones.* She rushed to get dressed, knowing full well that Peter still hadn't moved.

Frank appeared near the stream, rounding a large boulder. She was still topless, bent over, with her panties just past her knees.

He said nothing: Just looked from her to Peter, then back again. His expression didn't change, and he seemed... curious. Then, a moment later, he was gone, striding away into the trees.

Peter got to his feet finally, all the while watching her get dressed.

"That was strange," he said.

Yes, it was.

The memory faded. Another incident, strange but not really remarkable, amid the adventures of their journey into space and back.

She slept.

Chapter 15

EL-ICK

The Dreadnought *Scar* dropped out of leap space. Admiral El-ick watched as Alpha Centauri Prime came into view on the ship's forward screen. The sub-leap engines blazed a course for the human colony world. He hoped to destroy all of it, leave no trace, but he knew the task was impossible. So did Earth Command, but they conducted missions like this every month to keep the accursed living from building a fleet of their own capable of threatening Earth. His actual job was merely to weaken them and intimidate them into staying on their side of space until Earth Command finished assembling its armada to strike at the colonies, all of them, not just Alpha Centauri Prime, and end humanity for eternity. Two destroyers, the *Wound* and the *Maggot*, accompanied the *Scar* on this run. He smiled, seeing five human battleships racing from the planet's orbit to intercept them. El-ick leaned back in his command chair and ran the tip of a finger down the smooth flesh of his nearly flawless face. He wore his dark hair ragged and unkempt, but otherwise he looked the epitome of a conqueror. El-ick's body was lean and tight with muscle, enhanced by cybernetic filaments. He wore his gray uniform. His teeth were white and showed no imperfections.

El-ick's sharp green eyes were full of excitement as he spoke. "Have *Wound* and *Maggot* deal with the battleships. Put us on a course for the planet. Maximum thrust."

The human vessels opened up almost at the exact moment the destroyers launched their first waves of missiles. The space between the opposing ships filled with nukes burning towards their targets. "Countermeasures," El-ick ordered, knowing the humans would've targeted *Scar* above the other two ships under his command. *Scar* wasn't the flagship of the Earth's fleet, but she was one of the largest and most advanced to be constructed by rotting hands. Most of the ships in the Earth's fleet were older human vessels pulled from out of the mothballs, but the number of ships like the ones under his command were growing. The dead worked around the clock trying not only to build their own but to make them better than the ones gained from the remains of the extinct human civilization of the Earth. A pulse of energy sprang from the *Scar's* forward arrays, rendering the bulk of the incoming human missiles inert. The *Scar's* rail-guns took care of the rest as the massive dreadnought closed on the human fleet. *Maggot* was not so lucky. She took a nuke to her port side, which tore a hole in her hull. If she had an atmosphere, it would be leaking into space. The dead rarely bothered with any form of life support on their warships beyond pumping in heat to keep them from freezing in the void of the stars. There was no point. They did not take prisoners often.

Three of the human vessels took severe damage from the exchange. One of them flared like an exploding star as it broke apart and ceased to exist. A second changed its course, veering hard to port, to flee before El-ick's fleet. The battle continued to rage around the *Scar* as El-ick eyed Centauri Prime. The humans didn't appear to be building ships in space any longer. Space Docks were too vulnerable to attack without extreme orbital defenses like those around Earth. Planet based shipyards seemed to be all they had left.

El-ick motioned at Dirk, his first officer. "Scan for the largest shipyard and turn it into a heap of slag and ashes."

"Yes, sir!" Dirk nodded, his fingers dancing over the controls of his console. *Scar's* eighty launch tubes spat nukes at the planet in a seemingly unending stream. One of the human destroyers ran from the battle, racing the missiles towards the planet. El-ick watched a dozen leap points flickered on the screen. More human ships had arrived to join the fight. Though the prospect of taking them all on appealed to him strongly, he fought the urge down. Someday, they'd fight that last battle. "Order *Wound* and *Maggot* to recall their fighters! We've done enough here. Take us home!"

The three dead vessels flashed and disappeared from the space near Centauri Prime as the human battleship chasing the missiles aimed at the planet flew itself into the nuke's path and vanished in a ball of flame taking most of the strength of the attack with it leaving only a handful to rain down upon the world. Within seconds, they could see the mushroom clouds of nuclear detonation on the surface of the planet below.

Chapter 16

PETER

When the guards came, all three of them were awake. Frank was leaning against a wall, and Peter and Claudia were sitting on a bunk.

There were three guards and a fourth man. Two of the guards were Vic and Jimmy, and the third was someone new. They wore the familiar black bio-armor and carried assault rifles.

The fourth man was about six feet tall with a medium build and wore a baggy brown jumpsuit. His pale skin, wherever it was visible, appeared slimy or greasy. *Maybe sweat?* Whatever the stuff was, it coated him, glistening on his high cheekbones and in his crewcut hair.

"I'm Doctor Haiche, Doctor Gallows' assistant. I'm here to take some tissue culture samples."

"When are we going to get some answers, Doctor?" asked Peter.

"You aren't, I'm afraid, Mr. Hoyle. Time is brief now, for you and your friends."

"Then why are we still alive? Why spare us?"

The doctor grinned, revealing a mouth full of enormous yellow teeth. "Well, as I've mentioned, the samples, and then you will provide some sport."

Haiche stepped close to Peter, holding some sort of instrument that just fit into his hand. "Let me see your arm."

Peter looked at Claudia, Frank, and then back at Haiche.

"We can do this two ways, Mr. Hoyle, the painless or the painful, it is your choice for the moment." Haiche had a faint, supercilious smile on his face.

"Just give him your arm, Peter," said Claudia. "Get it over with."

Peter nodded, extending his arm toward Haiche.

The doctor ran the device over Peter's arm. A short, razor-sharp blade emerged. Without warning, he jabbed downward, gouging into the flesh of Peter's arm. Peter jerked and threw himself backward, blood spraying.

"Bastard! I'll get you for that!"

The guard, Vic, started forward, gun pointed at Peter. Haiche raised a hand. "Leave him be."

Vic stopped and frowned.

"Now you!" Haiche said while placing the bloody piece of Peter's flesh in a vial then stoppering it.

Claudia stepped forward and stood still.

Her eyes were closed. The extractor tool's blade cut through the fabric of her suit, passing across her belly. She swayed, shuddering as the cloth parted like tissue, revealing the smooth flesh beneath.

Peter stood still, feeling the sudden rush of blood to his cheeks, knowing his face was flushed. Claudia!

Vic was staring at him, hand on the big bore pistol. Peter could feel how badly the big man wanted to kill him.

Haiche's tool cut a path upward. Part of a pale breast appeared. The doctor slipped his hand inside.

Vic's hand pressed against his chest. Peter snarled, felt his adrenalin pulse and pound, and the gun was suddenly in his face.

"Do it, meat, come on. I want you to."

Haiche's arm jabbed and ripped free. Claudia cried out, falling away from him, but he fell with her. *I can't actually stand here and watch this! Must do something! Do or die trying!*

At that moment, Frank stirred to life, rushing over toward the struggling couple.

He grabbed the doctor's arm and twisted—The man's arm broke and Frank caught the tool in mid-air. Incredibly, Haiche didn't make a sound, even as Frank reversed the tool in his hand and stabbed downward, burying the blade into his forehead.

Vic shouted, turning away from Peter, lifting the gun. Frank threw the doctor's body and knocked Vic down. Frank followed, bellowing his rage, and threw himself at the remaining two guards.

Now is my chance! Peter stepped over beside Vic. As the guard pushed the doctor's body away, he drove his boot heel down onto his face. And again. Felt bones break.

Again.

Vic was no longer moving. Peter pried the pistol out of the man's hand. Then he unfastened the belt from around his waist. All the while, he kept his eyes away from the gory spattered mess.

Two shots dragged his attention back to Frank. He held a rifle in his trembling hands. One guard, Jimmy, lay sprawled against the wall with a bloody red halo spattering the wall behind him, and the other lay face down on the floor. Both looked dead.

"Oh dear God, Peter, we have to get out of here," said Claudia.

"Here, Peter," said Frank, "take a rifle."

Frank kneeled down and unbuckled the pistol belt from Jimmy's waist. He picked up the other rifle. Checked it over. Watched Claudia pick up the third rifle.

"The way I see it," Claudia said, "is we steal a shuttle or we get out of this building and into the city."

"The shuttle is the best option," Frank pointed out. "Let's go!"

Chapter 17

FRANK

F rank led the others through the winding corridors with dull gray walls, quite different from what he remembered. What happened to the human trait to make things more colorful and life affirming? The lifeless colors disturbed him. Could they fight their way out? How large was this building and how many people were in it? Up ahead, at the intersection in the corridor, was a terminal. He motioned for Peter and Claudia to stay where they were. He approached it carefully, peering around the bends. Once he saw it was safe, he examined the terminal. His fingers flew over the touchscreen, calling up a stream of data which rolled across the screen at lightning speed. His eyes scanned the words as they flew past. He located and memorized the layout of the building and the path to the shuttle docking area. Next, he pulled up everything from the computer's limited knowledge of the Earth itself. Luck was with him and he connected to an outside network via the terminal. No password needed. Fresh information scrolled down the screen.

"Frank!" Claudia whispered at him, urging him to move on. He disengaged from the system and turned to his friends. "We're in a lot of trouble. Follow me." He ran down the corridor.

Peter closed in, matching his pace. "What is it?" Peter asked, "What did you find out?"

"The Earth is dead. Humanity, as we know it died out years ago. A ship much like the *Hyperion* returned to Earth carrying a virus that killed everyone."

"What are you talking about? If everyone is dead, who were the guys we just killed?"

"They were dead Peter. I don't have time to explain. Just trust me, we need that shuttle. Escaping into the city isn't an option."

Chapter 18

EL-ICK

E l-ick sat behind the desk of his ready room, which was next to the bridge area of the Scar. The door slid open as Dirk entered. El-ick looked up at him, scowling. "What?"

"We've received news from Earth Command, sir."

El-ick set down the review of the ship's weapon upgrades he was working on. "What news?"

"The *Hyperion* has just come home, sir."

"The *Hyperion?*" El-ick asked. "One of the long range exploration vessels?"

Dirk nodded. "The crew was alive. Earth Command took them prisoner for study and fresh bio samples for the food-clone vats."

"My lord," El-ick whispered to himself. "That ship has valuable tech that was lost during the war. If the colonies get word of this, they may try to hit us whether they're ready."

"I don't think they'll be able to, sir. We hit them pretty hard on this run."

"Have you learned nothing about humans in all this time, Dirk? They aren't exactly creatures of logic. What we feel are but shadows of the emotions and passions that drive them. It's part of being alive. Emotion can be a powerful drive and throw things like logic and tactical readiness out the airlock in a situation like this."

El-ick stood up, heading for the bridge. "What's our best ETA back?"

"If we over burn the engines and risk damage, perhaps two hours."

"Make it sooner," El-ick ordered. "I want to see these humans myself before Earth Command hacks them up and hands them out in pieces and parts."

Chapter 19

CLAUDIA

S he held the rifle ready and looked outside.

The landing pad was empty.

The sun was out, shining strongly against the blue sky, and through puffy gray bellied clouds.

A sun-bleached stretch of concrete and steel awaited them, that, and a long drop to the ground below. *No way out this way, unless we're ready to end it all.*

The three of them stopped under what appeared to be an air vent. A humid breeze issued through the fragile, rusting panels. The ramp to the pad was just feet away.

"Back to the stairs," said Peter, leading the way back to the door.

The concrete steps of the stairwell crumbled occasionally under their feet as they descended. Ten flights down, Claudia could feel sweat on her forehead. A pale fibrous material crusted the walls that broke away in chunks whenever one of them touched it. Patches of black, oozing slime flecked the steps.

Claudia tried to stay calm, but a combination of everything she touched coated her hands. "I have to wash my hands," she said.

"We will get out of here, Claudia," said Frank. "Be strong."

"I'm just so miserable. Got gook all over me and I stink. I'd give anything to be away from here safe and clean."

The stairs never seemed to end, one flight after another, until she was a sweating, stumbling wreck.

"Two more flights, Claudia," said Frank. "come on, you can do it."

He's lying, trying to motivate me. Or Peter.

Peter looked miserable too, but he must have been saving his breath. He wasn't any steadier on his feet than her, and was leaning heavily on the rail as they descended.

Frank, other than being dirty, still seemed fresh and alert. What is with that guy—He's like a machine.

"I'm ok Frank, let's go."

Frank started back down and picked up his pace a bit. "Come on, we really are near the end."

Claudia and Peter followed him down the rest of the way.

"Smells like the sea," said Peter, "and something else."

At the bottom, the stair opened out past two long, rotted doors into a cavernous room. A scummy-looking green slime mold floated on top of four or five inches of the seawater that covered the floor. Here and there, the old floor tiles were still visible. Some sunlight came through a line of broken windows lining two sides of the room. *Must have been some kind of waiting room.* Couches, easy chairs and tables rose from the water covered with a thin sheaf of the green scum.

The water closed around their ankles.

Thank God my boots are insulated.

Frank walked across the room, sending a trail of ripples through the water. He stopped by one window and looked out. "We need to keep moving," he said, poking out a shard of glass from the window frame. He then stepped over the sill and outside.

Claudia hurried over and followed him, with Peter right behind her. All three of them stood on a sidewalk next to the overturned rusting hulk of a ground bus. A layer of mud had built up against the underside of the bus. A dozen small crabs darted toward holes and disappeared as she stopped near them.

The smell of the sea was even stronger outside. She could hear a seagull's lonely cry echoing off the walls of the surrounding ruins. They waded in. The water looked deep in places and covered the streets.

"Still know where we are going, Frank?" asked Peter. His rifle was now straddling both shoulders behind his head.

Is he ever serious about anything?

"This way," Frank said. "I'll go first. You follow behind Claudia... ok, Peter?"

"Sure thing."

Frank stepped off the curb, cautiously, found his footing and waded into waist deep water. Without thinking, Claudia forced herself to follow and felt cold water flow over the top of her boots and enter her suit through various rips and tears. The shock of it made her gasp, but it soon felt refreshing in the heat and mugginess in the air.

Wonder how filthy this water is? Clean or polluted? Worst part is not being able to see anything lower than mid-thigh. She held the rifle ready and felt the tension ratcheting her pulse rate up while waiting for something to burst from the water and eat her.

They tried to stick to the sidewalks.

Frank couldn't lead them straight to their destination. Too much rubble, with entire blocks of the city pulverized, and others impassable because of deep water. At last, though, they stood on a patch of dry ground in the shade of some immense oak trees. In front of them was a long sward of waist-high grass.

A block away was a line of warehouses and three starships: One shuttle; one atmospheric tug; and one that looked like an interstellar yacht.

In front of it all was a chain-link fence. Outside of the fence, a score or more figures were milling about: Shabbily dressed, ragged looking people. Several had a hold of the fence and were shaking it. Some were moaning loudly.

"This can't be good. Is that where you're taking us, Frank?" asked Peter.

Frank turned toward them with a bland expression. "Yes. Closest transport off planet. That yacht would be perfect. All the speed we need to escape anything short of a sunspot storm."

"Does sound good," Claudia heard herself say. Just thinking of the luxuries that might be aboard such a vessel was tantalizing.

"Those buildings," Frank said with a nod toward the warehouses, "are some of their cloning facilities. They clone people, and then infest them with a controlling parasite, or a sentient personality fragment of a long dead alien, if you will. These creatures have been at war with humanity before. One of our explorer ships, the *Cormorant,* had the misfortune of finding one of their homeworlds."

"You know a lot about them now, don't you?" Peter asked.

"Enough to horrify me, yes."

Claudia stepped forward next to Frank. "Let's get this over with. I just want to get out of here."

"Ok, Claudia, here's what I want you to do. Clear out any of the creatures that are in your way and make straight for the gate."

Claudia held up a hand. "How do we know those people aren't friendly?"

"Trust me, they aren't. Just listen! Blast open the gate if you have to, but head straight for yacht and get in. Peter and I will be right behind you, taking out the rest and watching for guards. Got it?"

Both she and Peter nodded, then all of them broke into a jog.

Chapter 20

FRANK

*A*ny hesitation is probably going to be fatal.

"Trust me, time is running out," Frank said.

Claudia and Peter nodded, but he could see the doubt on their faces when he asked them to trust him. *How to explain quickly, though?* Once Dr. Gallows knew of their escape, the pursuit would be immediate and deadly.

They're probably afraid, not distrusting.

As they drew closer, the stench of rot wafted to them on the breeze, then the detail of terrible, mortal wounds became obvious. *These people couldn't be alive, but they were.* The creatures weren't aware of them until they were scant yards away. In fact, Claudia dodged two and got right up to those around the gate before they could react. She fired repeatedly into them from behind, tossing bodies and limbs in a long, near continuous explosion.

For a moment, nothing stood between her and the gate.

Frank fired a burst from his rifle that sent three of them spinning, one losing an arm and another losing both legs. The third fell beneath the bodies of the first two. He spun to his right, snapping off several shots. One bolt hit a middle-aged re-animated man in the forehead and the other pinned a woman to a tree. *Must reach Claudia!* Even as he had that thought, he saw Peter go

61

down, falling over backwards in the tall grass beneath a woman. Everything slowed as he decided what to do. It was on him. Claudia had her back against the gate and was firing quick as she could as a ring of the creatures closed in.

Time ran out as he turned toward Peter.

Peter screamed, long and loud. *The woman was chewing on his arm!* Blood erupted onto the woman and sprayed the grass. *Too late, too late!*

Frank changed course, hoping to save Claudia. Saw with relief that the surrounding creatures were all down and she shooting the lock off the fence. He turned back toward Peter, barely stopping in time to avoid crashing into the woman.

She snarled up at him, as if to warn him off, as he raised the rifle high and slammed the butt down into her face. The horrible visage collapsed, crushed beneath the blow. Two more strikes put her down for good. Peter's features were gray, and his body was prone. *No time to think. Must hurry!* He scooped the other man up and slung him over his shoulder.

The gate was open. Claudia ran across a stretch of bleached concrete toward the yacht.

Frank followed, trailed by the remaining creatures.

Chapter 21

PETER

He awoke lying on his back on the warm concrete. His first instinct was to look at his injury, but he discovered the wound wrapped and his arm in a sling. He didn't want to see what the woman's teeth did to him, anyway.

The oddest sensation came from his wounded left arm: a wave of terrible itching worked its way through the veins of his ravaged arm and up into his shoulder.

He sat up, unable to stay still, and found himself on the floor of one of the warehouse buildings. *But why? Why aren't we on the ship getting the hell out of here?*

"Oh God," he heard Claudia say, "you look terrible, Peter!"

He tried to muster a grin. "Well, thanks a lot. Something's in me. I can feel it."

Frank stood nearby, looking at him. He said nothing, but Peter knew it was bad.

"Why aren't we on the ship?"

Claudia answered, "It has a magnetic lock. A magnetic field built into the landing pads holds all three ships in place. We have to find the control room to shut it off."

"Well, we better go then," he said, gritting his teeth, using his good arm to lever himself to his feet. He looked around and realized he must have dropped his rifle. The pistol was still there, though. He slipped it from the holster and released the safety.

Frank nodded, seeing that he was ready, and led the way deeper into the building. The front entry led to a room with boxes shoved against the wall and another door. Frank crossed over to the door with his rifle at hip level. The hum of machinery came through the door.

Frank opened the door and slipped through. Claudia motioned for him to follow. Peter knew he was a liability now, and would have to defer to them or risk getting them all killed. He followed as quick as he could, and entered a long, wide hallway, lined with several doors, each spaced about thirty feet apart. He joined Frank at the first door and peered through its built-in glass window.

The room held two rows of vertically mounted tanks, each containing the shadowy shape of a head, torso and shoulders. Surrounding each tank were various machines and instruments. There were a few gurneys, complete with tie-downs.

He didn't notice any attendants.

"Can't imagine any controls to the pad being there," said Claudia.

"No," replied Frank, "let's keep going."

The next door down was an airlock. The window revealed a chamber large enough for twenty people if they were friendly. "This doesn't look good either," said Peter. "We better hurry, too. I can feel whatever it is getting close to my neck."

"You can actually feel something inside?" Claudia asked, going pale.

"An itching sensation that burns. Who knows what it's really doing to me inside?"

Frank jogged ahead and glanced at the last door as they followed at a slower pace.

Bet I can't run now, even if I wanted to.

"This might be it!" Frank shouted, opening the door.

Frank ran inside over to a console. Overhead were ten monitors, each showing a different view of the facility grounds.

Frank flipped three switches, and three LEDs changed from active to inactive. "Has to be it!" he said, and once again resumed leading the way.

Another door with an exit sign was at the end of the hall. Frank told Claudia to go ahead while he helped Peter, as they all filed back outside.

"Just relax," Frank said. "Put your arm over my shoulder."

Frank lifted him into his arms like a bride. Despite his build, the feat came across as a too effortless.

"You augmented or something?" Peter asked.

"Something like that," Frank answered, nearly sprinting in his effort to catch up with Claudia. The door to the yacht was open. Frank lowered him to the ground so they could climb in, but that didn't slow them very much.

The engines whined as Claudia powered them up. Frank pulled the door closed while Peter settled into a seat.

Peter closed his eyes, finding it hard to believe they were actually pulling this off. Only the onward migration of the itching kept a smile off his face, that and a molten, acidic lump rising in his throat. "Oh Lord," he murmured, "what is happening to me?"

Chapter 22

EL-ICK

The *Scar* dropped into Earth space first. Space distorted, rippling, and then suddenly its massive form was there, where before there was nothing. The badly damaged *Maggot* and *Wound* appeared seconds later. Four other ships were already near Earth. Without consulting the sensor reading, El-ick recognized one of them immediately as the *Rot*. It was the vessel of the Lord Commander, Garok. The *Rot* was the most advanced battleship of the fleet, though it was smaller in size and power to the massive dreadnought he commanded. The other three vessels comprised the *Worm*, the *Grave*, and the *Entropy*. El-ick didn't have to wonder why so much of the fleet's main firepower had been called back to Earth. He could guess easily enough. Garok surely expected the colonies of Man to move against the Earth if they had heard of the *Hyperion's* return. Recovering its experimental drive tech alone would be worth the attempt but when it combined with the fact that it carried living humans and all the data stored within its systems of the ship's long voyage into uncharted space, an attempt at reclaiming it became a certainty.

"Open a channel to the *Rot*," El-lick ordered his comm. Officer. Garok's flawless pink face appeared on the screen in front of him. If El-ick himself looked almost human, Garok was the perfect picture of a living man his age. El-ick knew Garok was not only his superior, in command of the whole of the dead's fleet, but the most powerful unliving being on Earth, answering only to the council of elders that comprised the heart of Earth Command itself.

An eerie and condescending smile stretched over Garok's full lips as he saw El-ick through his own view screen. "Welcome home, El-ick. Glad you could join us. I have a feeling we will need the *Scar's* sheer power. There was not time to assemble more of the fleet. We are all that stands between Earth and the human fleet, which is reported on its way."

El-ick shook his head. "Garok, you know very well that even if ships were not present, the humans couldn't breach the Earth's orbital grid with anything short of a miracle."

El-ick watched as a crew member of the *Rot* handed Garok a mug of steaming blood where he sat in his command chair, then darted out of view. Garok sipped at the red liquid before he continued, unconcerned with making El-ick wait. "What you say is true, of course, but is the sport in it? Meeting them here is much more... arousing."

"There's no need to risk the ships of the fleet in this confrontation," El-ick warned him.

"If I want your opinion, El-ick, I will ask for it," Garok growled. "How badly damaged is *Maggot?* Can she stand with us?"

"No," El-ick lied. Her crew had been working to repair the *Maggot* so it could still fight if the need arose. Her crew had been laboring on in-flight repairs to her since the moment her last engagement ended. "She needs to be docked. A lucky shot could tear her apart."

"Fine," Garok waved dismissively. "Send her to one of the space docks inside the Grid's protection."

"This fleet, what do we know about it?" El-ick demanded.

Garok tapped controls on the arm of his chair. "I'm sending over the intel now."

El-ick looked down at the information uploading to the bridge's tactical screen. His eyes grew wide as he read the data. "Good lord," he muttered. "Are you sure this is correct?"

"Yes. The scout ship, *Cancer*, accidentally stumbled upon the human fleet in the sector where it was amassing. She transmitted this data via a Leap Space burst before being destroyed."

"If this is correct, this is almost the entire fleet of all the colonies combined and even some of the new ships they were completing. This makes no sense. Have the humans lost their minds?"

"Did you really believe anyone who still breathed was capable of rational thought or logic?" Garok laughed. "They are far too emotional to think clearly on any level."

El-ick leaned forward in his chair. "I request permission to take the *Wound* and whatever other ships you can spare back to the colonies immediately."

Garok smiled. "Request denied."

El-ick boiled with anger on the inside but kept it from showing on his face, or at least he hoped he did. "The colonies have to be almost defenseless, sir. There will never be a better time to strike them than now. It is without question, with so much of their strength headed here to engage Earth, the *Scar* alone could eradicate one of them. Give me a few ships and I will end this long war."

"Did you not hear me, El-ick? I deny your request. Now move the *Scar* and *Wound* into position with the rest of my ships so that we may face the humans together the moment they leap in."

"As you say, sir," El-ick answered, struggling not to show his utter contempt for Garok. "Do it," he ordered his helmsman. The *Scar's* massive, sub-Leap Space engines flamed and the enormous dreadnought moved to its place behind the Rot and the other ships under Garok's command.

Chapter 23

FRANK

"We've got two fighters on our tail, guys!" Claudia said over her shoulder while sitting in the pilot's chair. The yacht climbed rapidly into the sky.

Peter lay within the crèche of the robodoc. Frank looked up. "Do your best, Claudia. I think I'm losing him. He's got a fever, and the shakes!"

"It burns! Oh dear Lord, it burns! Help me!" shouted Peter.

Frank put a hand through the permeable field that surrounded the crèche, and on Peter's forehead. He was burning up and his face was ashen. A tremor racked his body, and then the machine's alarm sounded. Blood vessels burst in Peter's eyes, and his face went slack as he quit breathing.

Claudia cried out as she started a series of evasive maneuvers. Several of the ship's system monitors beacon'd in protest, adding to the cacophony.

A soft tone signaled an incoming message: "Attention the yacht, *Drachma*, we command you to stop and prepare to be boarded."

"We're about to clear the atmosphere, Frank. Half a minute more and we can leave these fools behind."

Frank didn't know what to say. It wasn't exactly a good time to tell her that Peter was dead. *The man's staring eyes were hard to take.* He had to do something, so he reached out to close his eyelids. He pressed down on the now cooling flesh and felt movement. The shock of it paralyzed him for a moment. He's dead! The robodoc's readouts supported this.

"Frank, they're shooting at us!" shouted Claudia.

A moment later, Peter grabbed Frank's hand, jerked it toward his mouth and bit down! *Ah, the pain!* He tried to jerk his hand free, but Peter was using both hands now and his grip was incredible. Frank watched the skin and fatty tissue of his hand peel away from the bone. With his left hand, he punched Peter and pulled his hand free. The pain shut down almost immediately, but the damage was done.

Oh, God! He thought and stared, holding his hand up. The bite exposed the Ferro-plasticized alloy composition of his hand with only shreds of flesh left hanging.

No hiding it now. Claudia would know that he wasn't human, but he didn't have time to worry about that.

Frank searched frantically across the robodoc's control panel, finally finding the lock-down button. He activated the field just as Peter was sitting up.

Claudia must have noticed something. She rushed across the cabin to his side. "What's happened? Oh no, look at him, Frank! His mouth is all bloody!"

"Make sure he doesn't get loose!" Frank ordered Claudia as he stood up, attention riveted to the yacht's alarm beacons screaming for attention. He hid his hand from view as he darted by her to the pilot seat. The *Drachma* had cleared the atmosphere, leaving the two atmospheric fighters behind and helpless to follow them. Frank's relief became terror as he stared out of the Yacht's front window.

"Oh God," he muttered. He hadn't worried about escaping through the Earth's defensive grid, a design solely to face external threats, but he had never imagined dealing with what he now faced. A battle larger than any he'd ever seen raged among the stars. A fleet of capital ships belonging to the dead squared off against an oncoming human armada. He jerked the craft's controls hard to the right, barely avoiding a missile as it blew past them towards a black destroyer. His super human synaptic speed combined with the Yacht's mobility was all that had saved them from becoming space dust. Then directly in his flight path: a ship so large that it blocked the stars from view as he approached its underside. It stretched over two miles long and was half that in width. The hull was midnight black streaked with silver and spotted with the scars of battle. It had to be a dreadnought class ship. Nothing else could be so huge. Double the size of the old *Julio Cesare* they'd encountered recently: an old first-rate heavy cruiser dwarfed by the new dreadnoughts like this behemoth. His heart sank as he realized it belonged to the dead. A human fighter darted past him on his approach, firing with all guns blazing into the thing. Fighter's fire didn't even penetrate the ship's armor and was nowhere near powerful enough to cause actual damage. The fighter continued straight on its course, hurling itself into the massive ship's hull. Frank blinked as the fighter exploded, leaving a hole where it had struck. Several bodies drifted into space from the opening. The big ship had no interior atmosphere or so little of one the rupture did not create the venting into space it would have done with a human ship. The tiny figures took potshots at the nearest human fighters with small arms as they floated further into the darkness.

Space itself seemed to shake, though Frank knew that was a trick of the human part of his brain, as the dreadnought opened fire on the human fleet. He watched the two human battleships explode. The surrounding battle was growing fiercer and many of the dead ships launched their own fighters now to engage the humans. *Drachma* had no significant armor. They needed to get away before a rogue shot took them out. He looked at the enormous dreadnought and knew what to do. *Out of the frying pan, into the fire. To survive, they were going to have to get aboard the thing.*

Frank used the yacht's sensors to find the dreadnought's fighter bay and set a course for it. The dreadnaught's fire focused entirely on the humans' capital ships. He believed that if the technology the dead used was akin to the human tech, he could safely get the yacht inside one of its bays. He punched up the yacht's speed and made his move.

Frank hated having no options. They would essentially hand themselves over to the dead once more, but given that option or the near certain fate of a fiery death in the battle's heart, he supposed surrendering at least left them alive with the chance they could escape again.

He flew the yacht straight into one of the massive ship's hangars at full throttle, cutting back his speed at the last possible moment. The sooner they got on board, the better. He watched the hangar personnel scatter as the yacht careened inside. The *Drachma* touched down on the metal of the hangar floor.

"Frank!" he heard Claudia screaming from where he had left her with Peter.

Chapter 24

KA-JHEA

Ka-Jhea gritted her teeth, and used maximum thrust to power her Hades-class fighter up and out of the launch tube. On either side of the fighter's main body, the wings expanded their delta shape as she swept through and switched to attack mode. Outside the cockpit: no sound; no screams; no gunfire; or explosions—Just huge silent fireballs, streaking missiles and crisscrossing beams of energy.

None of that mattered. Too much distraction came from her thoughts, anyway. She was monitoring both her own command channel and that of her enemy. Of course, just watching one of her enemy's capitol ships explode and imagining the sound of ten thousand humans screaming as one provided her with a music that had a unique flavor of its own.

"Incisor Sixteen, you have freedom of targets," said the voice of her commander from the command deck of the escort carrier *Pox*, or *Roma*, as the humans once called her.

"Order acknowledged," she replied, and cut hard right on a course that would take her beneath *Pox's* massive underbelly. A swarm of enemy fighters and gunboats conducted what appeared to be a suicide attack.

A list of potential targets immediately scrolled down in a transparent window just off center from her right eye, floating in mid-air. For the moment, the list included the closest targets, rather than by the level of threat they presented.

Her left hand trailed across the keyboard, selecting a trio of gunboats that were making a run at *Pox's* starboard, or right engine complex. They mounted an array of light defensive weaponry and two massive 300cm Hellbore cannons. A Hellbore could gut most ships at close range and specialized for close attack.

"Going in, pursuing three Hipper-Class gunboats, Incisor Command! Incisor wing, cover my six!" Her two wingmen immediately peeled away and sought the escorting enemy fighters.

As her small fighter closed within a kilometer of the deadly, mite-sized, but potent gunboats, she licked her lips, armed the missile array and settled her gunsight on the rear-most target. An acquisition signal beeped once, and she locked it down. One hundred uranium-tipped explosive rounds sped toward and through the closest gunboat and culminated in an out-of-proportion explosion that disintegrated all traces of the boat.

Next target acquired! The shimmer of defensive shielding made it a struggle to maintain even AI-controlled target-lock status. The enemy craft's twin turrets spun in their mountings, seeking her ship out. Another burst from her cannon penetrated and raked the gunboat. The resulting explosion flared and left a pall of smoke and swirling fiery fragments in its place.

One more! She pulled her fighter into another tight turn in her attempt to stay behind the third gunboat. This last target pursued his own agenda despite the death of his comrades. Both of his Hellbores blasted away at the *Pox's* launching bays, doing tremendous damage. The gunboat dodged right, and the cannons kept firing, trailing a line of destruction that must have reached stored fuel or ordinance in the landing bays. Several explosions shook

Pox's frame, and she realized that there would be no return for her there. The massive ship might even be in danger of a catastrophic explosion. She would hunt down this enemy.

The white-hot exhaust of the gunboat drifted into her sights. She locked her weapons onto it and opened fire. The Hades' cannons blazed away. She watched with delight as the gunboats' engines ruptured and split, leaking fuel before it exploded into a ball of light and fire. The battle drew to a close around her and the humans were turning tail. The remaining large ships entered leap space and vanished from the system. An alarm sounded. Her own craft had sustained damage. Her fighter needed to be repaired soon, or she might end up adrift and forced to endure a long and intolerable wait for a rescue crew to pick her up. She laughed as she noticed the closest ship was the *Scar*.

Ka-Jhea had heard tales of the mighty ship and its captain wasn't a captain at all, but an admiral who refused to leave direct command behind. "El-ick," she muttered.

Ka-Jhea opened a channel to the *Scar* and requested permission to come aboard. The *Scar* was the only ship of the fleet which hadn't launched fighters during the battle, but granted her request. Her fighter spun, curving in space, and streaked towards the massive dreadnought. With any luck, she'd find a new home there and eventually meet this "El-ick" so many living and dead alike feared. Then she saw it. *What the Hell?* she thought as a yacht darted into the dreadnaught's docking bay. *What was a civilian vessel doing in the middle of a space battle, much less going aboard Scar?*

Chapter 25

EL-ICK

The wait ended. The human fleet leaped into the system less than an hour later. Apparently, they had been in route behind the *Scar* and her support destroyers. Vast areas of the void rippled and tore as the human vessels emerged into actual space. El-ick counted over two dozen destroyers, all seven of the humans' known battleships, two fighter carriers, and several small frigates.

El-ick shook his head at the level of stupidity the living could sink to. *Rot* led the dead's own battleships and his destroyer, *Wound*, which Garok had assumed command of as part of the battle group, to meet them. The humans' weapons were already blazing. Nuclear missiles streaked across the void towards the dead fleet. Scores upon scores of single-man fighter craft were launching in a mad dash to reach the dead ships before they could deploy counter fighters. In this, the humans knew they had the upper hand. The living were faster than even the best of the dead in reflexive response times. It made them better pilots, and they liked to capitalize on this tiny advantage whenever they could.

El-ick scowled and pondered his course of action. He wanted no part of this battle. It was a waste of resources and an unneeded risk. The Earth's defense grid could easily handle anything this rag-tag fleet of human vessels could throw at it. Yet he could not simply stand by and do not nothing, watching his brothers meet true death. To end the battle quickly became his goal. "Helmsman, take us right down the humans' throats, full speed. Fire at will!"

As the first wave of human fighters reached the dead fleet and began strafing runs against the dead's battleships, the *Scar* rocketed forward. It moved between the two fleets, paying no heed to the small fighters swarming it. Tiny explosions danced up and down its sides as their projectiles struck its hull. *Scar's* railguns opened up first. Trails of projectiles cut their way through space, slicing two of the human battleships in half. Then *Scar's* missile tubes spat death into the human ships. One fighter carrier took over a dozen direct nukes and lit up like a fireball, taking a fresh wave of launching fighters with it. Three of the other human battleships also took hits, but none were severe enough to fully cripple them.

El-ick's eyes scanned the battle reports and sensor data being fed to the screen on his chair. So far, only one dead ship lost: The *Worm*, double teamed by two of the human ships, took the brunt of their volley fire and broke apart into pieces as their cannons blazed away.

El-ick held his fighters in reserve. He did not need to give the order from them to launch. It would take a miracle for the human fighter to do any actual damage to a vessel the size of the *Scar* and the other ships under Garok's command had already launched theirs. El-ick tapped into the comm traffic of the area and listened to the calm voices of the dead being atomized, and the humans screaming as they met death. Countless tiny blossoms of flame bloomed and vanished in the darkness of space. As he predicted, the dead fighters were vanishing by triple the number that the humans were. None the less, this battle belonged to the dead. He would see to that. He ordered his gunners to direct their fire solely at the lead human battleships. Within seconds, another exploded, and another one crippled. He could hear the cries of "Fallback!" and "Retreat!" being shouted over and over on the human frequencies.

A second dead battleship left this plane of existence as a nuke struck its primary engine and it went up like a white fireball into the surrounding ships. The human ships made the jump to leap space despite the minor victory of seeing another dead vessel destroyed. El-ick wondered how much damage they would have inflicted on Garok and his fleet had the *Scar* not been present.

El-ick nodded to Dirk to keep firing as long as they had targets. A stream of fire from one of the *Scar's* railguns tracked a human frigate and blew it to shreds just as its engines were reaching leap speed. El-ick noticed the human vessels were so desperate to get away, they were leaving many of their fighters behind. It was very unlike them. "Dirk, concentrate the railguns on the fighters. I don't want a single human left alive out there."

"Yes, sir!" Dirk barked back at him.

The humans paid dearly for their foolish act. They had lost four of their remaining battleships, seven or more of their destroyers, all the frigates that they had brought into the Earth system, and only God knew how many fighters. Much of this was the *Scar's* doing, and he was sure the legend of his massive and mighty dreadnought would continue to grow among the human in the colonies. Some of his own crew joked he was the lord of death. He could scarcely imagine what the humans must think of him.

Chapter 26

FRANK

The Drachma came to a stop, with Claudia yelling, and Peter trying to get free of his restraints.

Frank knew the dead outside the yacht would soon force their way in. "Claudia!" he shouted. "Forget about Peter and hide!"

Peter would be safe, although the dead virus infected him now. Soon he would be one of the enemy. They would likely let him live and enter their society. Claudia, however, was in great danger. The initial boarders would come in guns blazing, no doubt believing the yacht contained an assault force. He would meet them and give them the fight they were looking for. When they were done with him, Claudia's chances of survival would be much higher if they found her whimpering somewhere and not making a stand against them.

The yacht shook violently as an explosive charge detonated. Frank ran through the ship to the cargo hold. The enemy entered, shouting and cursing. Peter growled at him as he passed, flinging saliva into the air like a mad dog. Two of the dead stepped through the blown airlock into the yacht. He rushed them head on. He hit the first one so hard the impact threw the man back outside and sent him skidding along the hangar floor. The second attacker reached out to restrain him, but Frank caught his arm and snapped it off. Frank's hands found the sides of his head and, with a mighty twist, tore it from the soldier's shoulders. Frank felt a jolt as a stun dart embedded itself in his right arm. He shrugged it away.

Frank stopped in the doorway, facing a semi-circle of six more of the dead. Some were armored and others wore the work suits of engineers. Frank leaped from the yacht onto the closest of the dead. His fingers dug into the chest of an engineer and, with a heave, he ripped the man's rib cage apart and dropped the carcass on the floor.

A soldier struck Frank in the jaw with the butt of his rifle. Synthetic flesh tore along his cheek, exposing the metal underneath. He caught the soldier's weapon and jerked it from his hands. He shot him in the head, then shot two more.

Frank flew forward as someone delivered a kick to his back, which likely would have shattered a human's spine. He toppled face first to the metal floor and rolled to his feet. He faced a strikingly beautiful woman wearing a flight suit. Her skin was a light shade of gray but not decayed and her body was tight with toned muscle. She flicked long black hair from her face with a twitch of her head and stood with her left leg forward and her weight on her right foot. She beckoned him to make a move at her. The other dead backed off, content to watch what unfolded next. He lunged at her, swinging a hard right at her face. She ducked and came up with a jarring blow to his chin that left him stunned. She followed with a kick to his chest that knocked him down. Frank climbed to his feet, but the barrels of three rifles pointed at him. Frank held up his hands to surrender, but the thunder of their rifles deprived him of the option. His body bounced and spasmed as a slew of rounds blew holes in the flesh covering his true form and left dents in the metal underneath. His last memory before losing awareness was the female pilot laughing.

Chapter 27

CLAUDIA

F rank had told her to hide. Claudia could hear the sounds of battle raging outside of the yacht, and simply couldn't bring herself to follow his orders, though. She stood watching Peter struggle against his bonds.

"Oh Peter," she thought. "It's not fair. We finally make it home after all those years and the Earth is dead."

Peter leaned forward as far as he could and snarled at her with hungry eyes. His sudden move caused her to backpedal. As she did, the noise of armored boots clanking on the yacht's floor caused her to turn around. Two men in full body combat suits entered the yacht and moved towards her. "On the floor!" one of them ordered. Claudia had no choice but to comply. She raised her hands behind her head and sank to her knees.

"I surrender! My friend contracted the virus. Will you help him?" she pleaded, not knowing what else to do. The men laughed.

Chapter 28

EL-ICK

E l-ick stood before the mirror in his ready room with anger seething through every molecular cell of his form. Garok had crossed the line this time and the pink-faced bastard was filing court-martial charges against him and the crew of the Scar for not following direct orders during the battle with the human fleet. The man had sent him an encrypted message stating as much as soon as the battle had ended. "The fool!" El-ick raged and smashed his fist into the mirror, shattering it and sending shards of glass clattering to his feet. He looked at his hand and cursed himself for letting the anger get the better of him. The skin grafts to repair the damage he'd just done would not be cheap. He picked at the pieces of glass stuck in his flesh as he gritted his teeth. Like all the dead, except the extremely powerful and the council members who could afford direct sensory brain implants, he felt no pain. His nerves had long rotted away into nothingness. Had it not been for the actions of the Scar, the dead would have lost a great deal more in the skirmish, but Garok had a following and knew just the right ears into which to whisper his claims. El-ick would lose command of the Scar. It didn't matter that he was a legend among the fleet or that his years of loyal service and long lists of victories far surpassed that of Garok, a man who came to his position through bribery, murder, and cunning. El-ick understood Garok's line of thinking. The man wanted him gone simply because El-ick was the sole threat to his one day taking command of all the Earth fleet and the world itself. He knew Garok likely had a similar plan with which he would eventually depose of the council and become the emperor he longed to be.

El-ick weighed his options carefully. He could stand trial. In fact, it was his duty to do so and prove what Garok's motives for bringing the charges against him truly were or he could go rogue and take the Scar into deep space, leaving behind this world in order to keep his ship and perhaps one day return to see Garok face justice.

The military man in him wrestled with duty to the service and to the dead race that created them. He, Garok, all of them, a tool of vengeance, to the Imperative: the goal, the purpose that was supposed to matter, was the death of all humanity. El-ick knew this, but he would not allow Garok to take complete power. He would squander everything so many had perished to build since their race was born. El-ick nodded to himself and knew in that moment he would never surrender the Scar without a fight. She was his and his alone. The ship gave his existence purpose and meaning...

Was it madness to question what drove them all? The Imperative, my bond, my only love, this blood lust... that should unit us all.

The door behind him opened, and Dirk entered. "Sir, there's been an attempt to board the ship. I think you should come see what's happening in the hangar bay."

El-ick cocked an eyebrow at Dirk. He took a moment to gather himself, followed Dirk to the bridge, then to the lift down to the hangar bay.

"Sir," a bridge crewman said. "We have ships incoming!"

El-ick raced to his command chair and called up the data on the approaching ships. There were six assault shuttles with a squad of fighters flying escort en route to the Scar. He identified them instantly as part of the Rot's contingent. "Garok," he said the name aloud like a curse word, hatred and anger dripping from his voice.

"They're hailing us. They want to board us and I quote, sir, so that you can be properly relieved of command."

El-ick noticed Dirk cut his eyes towards him. The captain waited to see what his reaction would be. El-ick knew Dirk understood his philosophy the importance of the lives of the dead men and women of the fleet. Earth Command thought of them all as chess pieces, expendable. "Take us into Leap Space now!" El-ick ordered. "Maximum thrust!"

'Yes, sir!"

The stars rippled around the Scar and the enormous ship blinked away, leaving the shuttles and fighters behind.

Chapter 29

KA-JHEA

Ka-Jhea watched two armored soldiers drag the human female out of the yacht and take her away. The robot lay on the hangar, unmoving. Several more soldiers were cleaning up the mess from the fight and preparing to take it away as well. Most of the personnel in the hangar were still congratulating her on taking it down so easily. Engineers walked by, patting her on the back, and soldiers nodded at her with respect.

"What is that thing?" one of the older, decrepit engineers asked.

Ka-Jhea paused, not sure where the knowledge came from, and answered, "It's a class X3 android used on extended space missions to monitor the crew or to make sure there was someone there to get the vessel home if the crew fell to a radiation storm, virus, or the like."

"Humph," the old man snorted. "I thought all those things destroyed."

"Apparently not," Ka-Jhea smirked. "The bugger sure knew how to fight. I heard rumors among the fleet that the deep space exploration vessel the *Hyperion* had returned with its crew intact. I would bet that thing came back with them."

"There's an infected human on the yacht too," the old man grinned. "Have you gone in there to see him yet?"

Ka-Jhea shook her head in the negative. "I hear they're trying to decide whether to put him down or send him to the pens with the others ferals."

She looked at the old man, clearly confused. "I thought admiral El-ick didn't keep ferals aboard the *Scar*."

"He doesn't," the old man confirmed. "I meant shipping him over to the vessel that keeps the animals on board for ground combat. The *Scar* doesn't do ground combat. It doesn't need to. If our ship shows up in orbit, you can bet the humans best be crapping their pants and praying they got enough orbital defenses or ships to get us to go away. They know the *Scar* can and will just kill them all from space. It's what we built this beautiful monster of a lady for," he finished, waving a hand around at the walls of the *Scar's* hull.

Ka-Jhea watched him hurry away to help with the repairs on her fighter. She wandered through the area of the hangar bay, looking for the deck officer. She needed to check in and make sure that he allowed her to sign on as part of the *Scar's* complement. This was a chance that only came along once, and she knew it. There was no way she was going back to another ship if she could somehow stay here and serve under El-ick. She longed to meet the man who had become such a legend. On this ship, she could truly make a difference in the war effort against the colonies under his command. Unlike Garok and many of those in Earth Command planet-side, El-ick wanted the war over and was often too vocal, in her opinion, about the need to destroy humanity quickly. While she was aware, he was in favor of wiping out the humans to fulfill The Imperative; she wondered just how far he would go to see the dead under his command stop meeting the true death. She set herself up to be disappointed with her high, perhaps even unrealistic, expectations of the man, but she couldn't help it.

Ka-Jhea spotted the deck officer standing in a group of engineers, giving reports on the battle damage the *Scar* suffered. *Time to secure my posting.*

Chapter 30

RON

C aptain Ron Davis watched the two suns of the Alpha Centauri system as he sat at the fortified post atop the hill
overlooking the spaceport. Alpha Centauri Prime was home to
over seven million living souls and the heart of the remnants of
human civilization. The city of New Charlotte was a gleaming
testament to what mankind was capable of at its best. The high
spires of towering apartment and government buildings reached
into the blue sky. Air cars whined through the spaces between
them as the day progressed.

He'd heard the news of the of the home fleet's failure to penetrate the Earth's defenses. Losses to the fleet panicked people.
If the dead came calling now, defeat seemed certain. Humanity's
dreams were full of howling dead things running across the plains
of Alpha Centauri Prime towards the great city of New Charlotte,
with blood-smeared mouths and hungry eyes in numbers far too
great to be stopped.

Ron lit a cigarette and puffed on it. He wiped away the sweat
on his forehead with the back of his hand. The suns were hot
today. He exhaled rings of smoke up at the cloudless sky. It was
a nasty habit and one that was mostly long dead. He had to grow

his own tobacco just to keep doing it. He was well aware of the social stigma attached to the habit, but didn't care.

Private Chad Morris came sauntering up the hill to the lookout post where he sat. Ron smiled at the private, glad to see relief arrive. His shift had stretched over twelve hours as it was, and he needed a drink. The private saluted, and he saluted back as soon as he got to his feet. He collected his rifle from where it leaned beside him. The people of the city demanded watches and out-posts in case the dead slipped into the sector unnoticed. They had troop ships that dropped "feral" pods to the planet's surface. Ron's force had to keep the dead off until they could prepare defenses or the populace escaped. The ferals were the dead's shock troops. They had no other purpose. When the disease reanimated the dead and gave them life, it left them in a state of insanity, much like an animal driven mad with hunger. The thinking dead was the real enemy. The ferals were expendable infantry and nothing more.

Ron had fought ferals long ago when the dead began their as-saults on the colonies and overrun the Earth. He remembered the way the things stank and their gangrenous green skin peeling from their face at it rotted. Only a head shot stopped them. Anything less still left them dangerous, even if they were in pieces. Their howls haunted him in his dreams to this day.

Yep, it was definitely time for a drink; he thought.

Chad entered the small, roofless bunker. "Thanks," Ron said. "Make sure you stay alert. The big wigs are keeping a close eye because of the trouble in space. Got it?"

"Yes, sir," Chad replied.

Ron left and headed out onto the sand. He made his way to the base of the dune, where military grade, one person, ground-based APCs waited. He hit a button on his remote and the canopy of his vehicle opened as he approached. Ron slid into the seat and the vehicle sealed itself, establishing its own internal atmosphere. Cranking up the "AC" and his music, Ron kicked the APC into gear as an old Earth band called AC/DC rocked through the speakers. A cloud of sand flew into the air as the APC streaked towards the gleaming city of New Charlotte below.

Chapter 31

CLAUDIA

C laudia awoke screaming. Her yells echoed off the metal walls of the cell she lay in. The room was empty. There was no bed, toilet, or anything. An electro-field locked her inside. Her head ached like someone had smashed in her skull with a sledge-hammer. Slowly and gently, she used her arms to push herself up and make it to an upright position. It took her a moment longer to gather her strength enough to get to her feet. Finally, she rose and made her way to the bars. It was freezing, and the air felt thin. It was clear the dead had increased the almost nonexistent atmosphere of their ship to better accommodate her and keep her alive. Too bad the bastards can't feel well enough to know when it's freezing, she thought as the cold sank deeper into her bones and she rubbed at her arms as she hugged herself.

"Claudia?" a strangely familiar voice asked from the cell across the hall. She couldn't make out his shape. The voice sounded like Frank, but was off somehow, with a metallic sound to it.

"Frank?" she asked. "Is that you?" The figure got up and came closer to the cell's bars.

"Yes, it's me, Claudia," he answered, and stepped into a bar of light.

She gave a little gasp. Why am I so surprised? Not like I didn't know androids existed.

"So many secrets Frank, I don't really know you at all, do I?"

"I guess not."

Just looking at him unnerved her. Nothing of the man she knew remained. Nothing of a man, either, she thought with a measure of sadness and disgust. Somehow, I knew. Must've been why I picked Peter. I knew. He's a thing. Not alive at all. If I close my eyes, Frank can still be a living person, and Peter won't be dead.

"I am distressing you. Think of me as a guardian, and it will be easier. I am an acquaintance."

"Yes, I see that now, but it's too much seeing you like this."

"I understand, Claudia. I tried so hard..."

"I know, Frank," she said, and forced herself to really look at him.

His true form, if you could call it that, was that of a pale Ferro-plasticized alloy known for its strength and malleability. Close to indestructible. His eyes were jade, and the nose a stub. No ears that she could see, no hair, just the pale psuedo-skin with its underlying, intricate tracery of veins, strands of muscle and tendon flowing through his body.

"My flesh wasn't salvageable with the virus loose in my flesh. Its taint could not reach my core, but it forced me to shed my shell. They know what I am. I lost the element of surprise. No escape for us this time."

"What about Peter? Did you—"

"I don't know what happened to him."

"Then he may still be alive?"

"I hope not, Claudia. Hopefully, he's gone. From what I understand of the dead, based on the information I scanned from their computer systems back on Earth, they go through a period of being feral, hunger driven monsters at first. This period can last months, depending on the person. The thinking dead look down on these feral monsters with little regard for their lives. Assuming Peter lives through the feral period, it is likely he will regain his intellect, but not necessarily any recollection of who he was when he was alive. Some do and others do not. Regardless, he will be like a child, learning and growing as his mind slowly turns on once more and his powers of reasoning increase."

"Where do you think they took him?"

"They keep the ferals in pens or cages and use them as shock troops for the dead's navy and armed forces. However, given our proximity to Earth, it is possible that they have shuttled him back to the planet to let him develop into one of the thinking dead hoping he will keep his memories and be able to share his knowledge of the Hyperion, its mission, and drive tech with them."

She leaned against a wall and slid down into a seated position. She closed her eyes.

Chapter 32

EL-ICK

Dirk stood beside El-ick in the lift as it shot down towards the ship's brig to visit the unexpected intruders locked inside the ship's detention cells. "Garok isn't just going to let us go, sir."

"Stop," El-ick said. The ship's AI ordered the lift to come to a halt. He turned to Dirk. "Garok is and always has been a fool. The man thinks of nothing but himself and personal gain."

"You should have made a move against him before now," Dirk stated.

"Politics is not my concern. I have no desire for power beyond that. I need to help protect our world and our race, but I will not stand idly by anymore and let Garok throw away all we have worked for since our race was born."

"Garok has the upper hand now, sir. Your inaction and faith in our people to deal with him on their own has left us in a much weaker position. You disobeyed his orders during the skirmish with the humans. The *Scar* was supposed to hold back while his ships engaged them."

"You know as well as I do how many of us I saved from the true death by disobeying Garok's idiot orders!"

"Indeed, sir, I do. I agree wholeheartedly with your actions. I do not believe that the Over-mind shall see it that way. Perhaps in the early days, before we got the clone machines online and could propagate our species, yes, but now, they will not care how many you spared. The navy, like the ferals, is expendable as long as Earth herself stays safe. They will back Garok's claims and he will come for us with everything he can muster."

"The *Scar*..."

"*Scar* is an awesomely powerful ship, sir, but it is not indestructible."

"Dirk," El-ick warned, "do not talk down to me as I were Garok. I know full well the danger we face, and also know we cannot run forever. We will devise a way to deal with Garok and get out of the current mess. I assure you. Now, I believe we have prisoners to deal with, yes?" El-ick changed the tone of his voice and spoke to the lift. "Resume," he ordered, and their journey to the brig began again.

As the lift doors opened and the pair stepped out into the security level, Dirk took the risk of angering El-ick further. "May I at least ask where we're headed, sir?"

"Alpha Centauri," El-ick answered with a wide grin as Dirk stared at him in total shock.

Chapter 33

FRANK

F rank sat on the single bunk in his cell. He did not truly need to rest in the human sense; it was just more comfortable for him at the moment: Habit, really. Claudia had withdrawn into herself. Whether it was from the loss of Peter or the shock of his own revelation, he couldn't say. She lay on the floor of her own cell, curled up into a ball.

The cell door opened, and two armored guards stood at attention as two other men entered and approached him. Both were dead, of course, but one of them looked passably human. His face had no obvious signs of decay and his movements were as graceful as a cat's. He wore an admiral's rank on his uniform collar. The man beside him, a captain, younger in appearance, although not in as good of shape. His skin was sickly, pale gray and his eyes were red, filled with dried blood. The admiral walked to his cell and stood in front of the field. He wore a sardonic grin.

"My name is Admiral El-ick. You are currently aboard my ship, *Scar*. I need to know who you are and why you came aboard my ship. I will ask only once."

"I am a class X3 android designed to..."

"I know what you are," El-ick cut him off. "I want to know who you are."

"My name is Frank," he started again. "I am from the deep space exploration vessel called *Hyperion*. We were on a five-year mission to explore beyond the boundaries of known space. We returned home to find your people in control of the Earth. I freed myself and two of those under my protection. Using a stolen yacht, we left the Earth and found ourselves in the middle of the recent space battle. I saw no choice but to seek shelter and your ship was the best option available to me. We boarded you to surrender rather than face certain death in space."

"I see," El-ick said. "One of those under your care is a feral. My security personal has him locked in a cell such as yours for his own protection. It appears his reaction to the virus is... abnormal. However, I confess, it has been so long since an actual human has undergone the change where we could observe it. Who can say with certainty what effect it has on a human not grown in a vat?"

Frank noticed Claudia sitting upright, listening to the conversation he was having with the dead men, but had not joined it. "So, Peter's alive?"

El-ick laughed. "As much as I am."

"Can we see him?" Claudia asked. Frank watched as El-ick turned toward her, acknowledging her existence for the first time since entering the cell block. "Trust me, you would not wish to. He is feral and dangerous. Perhaps, as time progresses, a visit is possible, assuming you are still alive yourself."

Frank moved next to the bars of his cell, drawing as close to El-ick as he could without appearing threatening. "What do you want from us?"

El-ick titled his head as if surprised by the android's question.

"Clearly, you want something or we would be dead already," Frank added.

"You are correct. I need something from you. We are on our way to a world called Centauri Prime. Because of circumstances beyond my control, I find myself in need of, what do you humans call it, asylum?"

"And how are we to help with that?" Frank asked. "I have not seen a human outside of the *Hyperion's* crew in five years. We barely know anything about your war and the state of the galaxy. I know nothing about Centauri Prime."

"True, but I imagine they would take my request much more seriously and believe it if you and your human companion vouched for my ship and my crew."

"Why would we do that?" Claudia snapped. "You're all monsters, rotting sacks of soulless flesh that should go back to Hell screaming."

"You're still breathing, are you not?" El-ick moved to stand outside her cell. "I offer you freedom for you all if you help me. Besides, if you do not help, not even *Scar* can tackle the entire remnants of the human battle fleet alone. You will die in the cold, dark void of space along with myself and my crew, as the humans scramble everything they have left to destroy us and this ship."

"If we help you, what happens to Peter?" Claudia demanded.

"I don't care. You may take him with you if you like, though I highly doubt your kind will allow him to continue to exist. The danger of the virus getting loose in their cities would be too great."

"We'll help you," Frank said. He shot Claudia a look, hoping she wouldn't argue. "We accept the terms of our freedom and Peter's in trade."

"Wonderful," El-ick smiled. "We should arrive at Alpha Centauri Prime within the next few hours. I will have you brought to the bridge before then so we can plan how to approach the humans to best ensure survival for us all."

With that, El-ick and the subordinate officer left. Frank watched Claudia closely. He could see the hope returning to her eyes.

Chapter 34

PETER

Peter awoke hanging on a suspension web. It kept him from damaging himself while in its restraining grip. There were no words capable of describing his pain. His thoughts were slow and cloudy. He struggled to remember who he was and what was happening to him. Peter's bloodshot eyes made their way around the room, taking in the empty black space. The room was dark, and he was alone. A fresh wave of hunger hit him and he tried to scream at the pain, but all that came out was an animal-like howl. Flashes of memory sparked in his head. His name was Peter. Once, long ago, it seemed, he had been a man. What he was now, he didn't know. Was this his home? No, he'd been trying to escape, get free of something beyond the bonds which held him, but he didn't know what. He recalled a woman. He could see her clearly in his memories, where so many other things were hazy or merely gone. Her name was... Claudia. Yes, that was it, Claudia, and she needed him. He struggled and squirmed, trying to twist free. He gnashed at the web with his teeth.

Peter looked up, snarling as the door to his cell opened and a man entered. The man wore black combat armor, but no helmet. His face was a mess of rotted flesh and wounds that would never heal. Peter watched as the man looked him over. Finally, the man spoke in a cold, hollow voice. "Do you know your name?"

Peter strained to speak. "P-P... et... er."

"Impressive," the man commented. "It takes most ferals months to even understand what's being said to them."

Peter relaxed in the suspension web, hanging limply in its embrace.

"Well, Peter, you are aboard a ship called the *Scar*. My name is Reaper, and I'm in charge of *Scar's* marine unit. I'll give you a choice. I will draw my sidearm right now and send you on to the next life or you can join my men and learn how to be a person again, not just an animal ruled by the hunger you're feeling. Which do you want?"

"L... e... Learn," Peter got out the word, though it took all his will to do so.

"Good," Reaper smiled. "I will give your mind a bit more time to finish waking up, then I'll return so we can start your training." Reaper spun about and marched out of the room, leaving Peter alone in the darkness once more.

Chapter 35

RON

New Charlotte's defense sirens cut Ron's R&R short. He had a comfortable seat at the bar and his hands on an ice-cold beer when the high-pitched wails began. His helmet's personal comm link went off. He put the helmet back on and answered, "Go for Davis!"

A tiny image of a cadaverous one-armed man, General Ackerman, shimmered into existence on his Heads Up Display. "Captain, report to your post immediately."

"On my way there now, sir! What's going on?"

Ron listened to a terse explanation of what was happening in space, signed off, and drank the beer. He dashed for his vehicle.

Chad was still on watch when he arrived at the lookout post. "I heard the alarms. Do you know what's going on, sir?" he asked.

"It's the *Scar*," Ron answered. "Long range scanners say she's in Leap Space on her way here."

Chad went pale. They both knew there were only two ships currently in orbit around Centauri Prime, and one of those was undergoing massive repairs from the failed attack on Earth. "I thought..." Chad started, but Ron cut him off mid-sentence.

"Yes, Private, The *Scar*. The one and only dreadnought in existence, okay?"

"My God..." Chad muttered. "Why are they even bothering to scramble us, then? The *Scar* has never used a ground attack. It's just going to sit up there and pound us all to Hell."

"Because, Private, we're grunts and it's our fate to die out here alone. It's our job."

Chapter 36

EL-ICK

E l-ick sat in his command chair as the *Scar* entered normal space and its standard thrusters kicked in. The massive dreadnought was fifteen minutes away from reaching orbit around Centuri Prime. He watched on the ship's view screen as a single human battleship moved to intercept them. It was hard not to laugh as he wondered what the poor, living commander of it must be thinking in this moment. He did not envy the man.

"Open a channel to that ship," El-ick ordered. "I want a chance to talk to them before we're forced to blow them out of the stars."

The face of a man in fifties with short cropped gray hair and blue eyes appeared before El-ick. "This is Captain Blane of the Battleship *Griffin*. I order you to leave this space or we will engage you."

Good, El-ick smiled inwardly. The man did indeed know he had no hope against the *Scar*, even with Centuri Prime's orbital defense grid to back him up. The captain was desperate enough to talk, and that was exactly what he wanted. "This is Admiral El-ick, in command of the Earth ship, *Scar*. I suggest you power down your weapons unless you really want to see what my ship is capable of. We've come seeking asylum."

Those words went against the grain of The Imperative. It would be a test of his crew's loyalty, but maybe not. The Over-mind was old, and the unity of purpose that swept them to victory on earth seemed not so strong now. His squabble with Garok evidenced the decline.

Blane was stunned to silence. El-ick could see the utter shock in his eyes. Never had a dead vessel requested human aid, and the *Scar* was far from an ordinary dead ship. She was a legend. "Say again?" the captain asked.

El-ick leaned forward, closer to the screen. "I request sanctuary and refuge in human space. I am prepared to offer my ship to the defense of your world should the need arise."

The captain of the human ship clearly thought he was lying, but there was hope, the hope of a man who seconds ago faced certain death and found a chance to live clear in his expression. "How do I know this isn't a trick?"

El-ick motioned for Claudia to be brought forward into view of the screen. "This is Yeoman Claudia Coyne from the old Earth ship, the *Hyperion*, which recently returned to Earth. She will attest to the sincerity of my claim."

"He speaks the truth, Captain Blane. I am one of three, er, I mean two survivors from *Hyperion*."

The captain looked at something off-screen. "Yeoman Coyne? We show you in the crew's complement for the *Hyperion*, and your voice matches your record. How did you end up aboard the *Scar*?"

"Upon our return home, a decon unit boarded the *Hyperion* and took the ship by force. They slaughtered most of us and made the rest prisoner. They took us to Earth to be processed. Two of us escaped thanks to the efforts of the X3 android assigned to our ship. However, as we fled in a stolen ship, we found ourselves caught in the middle of your attack on Earth. Were it not for admiral El-ick, we'd be dead. I've spoken with him at great length. I believe his offer is sincere."

El-ick watched as she spoke the well-rehearsed script they agreed on.

The captain looked as if he did not know how to respond to the unimaginable events unfolding before him. "I will need to consult with our president. In the meantime, hold your current position and do not approach the planet."

Blane signed off and the *Scar's* view screen reverted to an image of his ship which held its own position between the *Scar* and the world of Centauri Prime.

"You did well," El-ick said to Claudia. "If he grants my ship sanctuary, you will be free and among your own people once more."

Claudia said nothing. El-ick motioned for the guard who had accompanied her to the bridge to lead her back to her cell. "Thank you," El-ick offered, despite Claudia's coldness. The woman was rather fetching, and he respected her strength in such dire circumstances as those she'd faced on Earth and aboard his ship.

As soon as she left the bridge, El-ick waved for Dirk to approach him. "The *Hyperion*, is it still in orbit around Earth?"

Dirk nodded. "It was when we left the system. I imagine it's still undergoing study at the space dock they assigned it to upon arrival."

El-ick's lips parted in a smile. "Dirk, I want you to prepare and an assault team. We have three shuttles outfitted with the new smaller Leap drives. Go back there and bring me that ship."

Dirk stared at El-ick. "Sir?"

"You heard me, captain," El-ick ordered more firmly. "I want it here by tomorrow. Take as many marines as you feel you need."

Chapter 37

REAPER

R eaper stood in the training area, yelling at the men who were sparring to keep their hand-to-hand skills sharp as he pushed them on. Reaper would've blinked in surprise as the captain entered, but his eyes lids had been gone for years, burned off by a close call with a human grenade during the last days of the conflict for the control of the Earth. He snapped to attention as Dirk approached him. "At ease, commander," Dirk ordered. Reaper relaxed by a tiny fraction. "To what do I owe the pleasure of this visit?" he asked.

"I need you and two dozen of your best. The Admiral has deemed it fit for us to return to Earth via shuttle and steal the old Earth ship the humans came home in."

Reaper whistled. "He does like impossible tasks, doesn't he? They guard that ship heavily. If I understand correctly, Earth Command desperately wants its proto-type drive. I am sure they've already assigned several science and engineering details to look at it and how it functions aboard the ship. In fact, there's no guarantee that they haven't already gutted that ship sir and took the drive back to Earth to study. What does he expect us to do if we get there and take the thing, only to be stuck with no way to leap out of the system after we have her?"

Dirk shrugged. "He's El-ick. I imagine he expects us to perform a miracle."

Reaper grunted. "I'll get my team together. How long do we have?"

"I will lead this mission personally," Dirk informed him. "I want you and your men waiting in the *Scar's* port hangar bay in less than an hour."

The three shuttles dropped out of Leap Space close to Earth's moon. Twin missiles streaked from each shuttle, targeting the small outpost on the surface. The structure erupted into a ball of fire and flying shrapnel. Reaper let out a cry of triumph where he stood above Dirk in the pilot's compartment. He noticed Dirk's grin.

"We're all clear," Dirk said.

Reaper nodded, "Phase one, complete."

The outpost was the only monitoring station on the dark side of the moon and they were now totally invisible to the Earth unless they had the bad luck of an actual warship passing by them during their stay and they didn't plan to stay long. Long enough to punch in a new set of coordinates and make the last jump into the space dock which held the *Hyperion* its self. "This plan is crazy," Dirk commented. Reaper laughed, "It's your plan, sir." "I know. Why do you think I am so scared?" Dirk joked back, trying to break the tension. "Locking coordinates now." Dirk's fingers flew over the shuttle's controls. The plan was to leap into the docking station, literally. The combat shuttles' heavy armor would protect them, they hoped, while the disturbances hit the dock like a series of nukes. Reaper figured Dirk thought this would leave them in a state of shock while also inflicting heavy losses on the station's personal. Their team would ditch the shuttles, which would be useless and barely hanging together after such a stunt, and head directly for the *Hyperion*, shooting anything in their path that so much as moved. Once aboard, they'd fire up the old ship's engines and get the hell out before the Earth Command troops even knew what was happening. Dirk finished his programming and activated the leap drive. The shuttles blinked out of normal space once more.

This time, when the shuttles dropped out, it threw Reaper all the way back through the ship to bounce off the rear wall. His heavy armor clanged as metal struck metal and he landed face first on the floor. He pushed himself up, spitting teeth. "Damn it!" he cursed. The shuttle's aft door opened behind him as he leaped to his feet and followed Dirk and his men out. They were all lucky to still be existing. The shuttle looked like a mangled dog toy. The area inside of the surrounding dock looked even worse. He could see stars through holes in the station's walls and truly dead Earth personal floated in their path, twisted and broken bodies careening this way and that in the now zero G environment. If the station had contained a real atmosphere like the ones humans used, they would have all vented into space. Reaper didn't have time to be thankful, though. His armored feet thudded along as he took the lead, passing ahead of Dirk, and shouted, "This way!" He rounded a corner in the labyrinth of corridors leading to the *Hyperion* and came face to face with another dead soldier. Before the man could raise his weapon, Reaper's highly experienced reflexes gave him the speed to put a round through the man's head. The soldier's helmet shattered as chunks of meat and gore blew out the backside of his skull.

Reaper noticed the rookie, Peter, right beside him. He didn't like that a bit, but what was he to do? The boy was too fresh in his unlife for him to have felt good about leaving him on the *Scar* without being there to make sure Peter stayed out of trouble, but now Reaper wondered if he'd made a mistake. If the boy screwed up here, they'd both die for it. They reached the airlock at the same time as a team from one of the other two shuttles under the command of one of Reaper's most trusted warriors, Pus. Pus motioned for them to get back as he placed an explosive charge on the airlock door leading into the *Hyperion*.

"We lost One Eye and the other team. Their shuttle didn't make it!" he yelled, then ran towards cover as the timer on the charge ticked down. A deafening explosion rocked the hallway as the airlock door imploded. Then they were all moving again, racing aboard the ship they'd came to take back with them. A stream of the space dock defenders caught up with them. The marine next to Peter fell, his body nearly sawed in half by the blast from a high-powered gauss rifle.

Reaper said, "Pus, I need your team to hold them!"

"Roger that!" Pus shouted. He spun and opened fire on the closing troops. His team fanned out, taking cover wherever they could.

"Dirk!" Reaper screamed, "Come with me! We need your ass on the bridge getting this thing fired up yesterday!"

"Wait!" shouted Peter, "I can help."

"Then get a move on! Move it! Move it!" Reaper shouted. He knew Peter was originally from this ship. If the man had regained his memories, this could be a lot easier than they thought it was going to be.

Chapter 38

PETER

The guy they called Pus pulled him through and sealed the outer lock and inner lock doors. "They follow us through there and the game's over."

There wasn't time to reply. Reaper was shouting.

Something still felt off inside, but mostly, he ran smoothly, and he knew *Hyperion* better than anyone. *She's mine. And always will be! These guys just don't know it yet!*

Dirk exited the grav tube, and Reaper followed on his heels. Peter led the way, passing the others in a mad dash for the bridge. He knew he could access everything he needed in engineering from there.

They encountered little resistance aboard, and Reaper and his men made quick work of anyone who stood in their path. As soon as they hit the bridge, he and Dirk took over. Peter ran to the engineering console. The drive was still on board and functional. With a few keystrokes, he brought it online while Dirk took the command chair. "All systems go," Peter said. Dirk grinned at him and Peter nodded. Peter redirected the helm to the command chair. The massive ship shook as it broke free of the mooring, holding it to the space dock.

"Incoming!" screamed a soldier who had taken the sensor console. "We've got fighters closing fast and two battleships breaking Earth orbit to intercept us."

Peter routed all the extra power he could into the ship's drive as Dirk pilot them away from the dock into open space.

"Is she ready?" Dirk asked.

It was Peter's turn to grin. "Oh, she's ready. Those poor guys don't have a chance." The *Hyperion's* engine was many times faster than any conventional military vessel's. She could make jumps in Leap Space at mind-boggling speed.

Dirk pressed a button, and the stars blurred around them before the battleships got weapons lock on them.

Chapter 39

EL-ICK

As the shuttle left the *Scar's* bay, El-ick sat comfortably in the rear passenger compartment, thinking. He was not in the slightest worried about meeting with the leaders of Centauri Prime face to face. If they made a move against him, the *Scar* would level their cities. The humans couldn't recall enough vessels to match the *Scar's* fire power fast enough to stop its rain of destruction. Besides, he knew he had an ace up his sleeve. Dirk should be returning soon with the *Hyperion* and then he would have two vessels under his command in orbit around the humans' planet.

The *Hyperion* was mainly a science vessel built for exploration but like all long-range ships of its era; she had weapon mounts. She had teeth, and she was super-fast for a ship her size in normal space. Her Leap drive was faster still. The ship would give the humans a huge tactical advantage in the war if they could copy its drive and install similar ones on their warships.

The shuttle swooped down through Alpha Centauri Prime's atmosphere, approaching the world's capital city. Through a window he studied the blue sky. He remembered when another planet, like Earth, had once looked like this back when he was truly alive. It reminded him of the beauty that was lost when his kind took power. Their reign over the Earth was a dark one, lacking the extent of personal freedoms that these humans held so dear. El-ick knew he was far more emotional than most of his race. It was both a curse and a blessing. It was part of what made him such a dangerous adversary to Garok. *Perhaps I am indeed getting soft in this decaying state.*

A white-haired man in blue robes stepped forward to meet him, extending a hand. El-ick sensed fear in him but also a determination to protect his people.

"Welcome to Alpha Centauri Prime, Admiral El-ick," the man said. "I am President Chapman, leader of the Terran Coalition, representing all the remaining worlds of man."

El-ick took his hand and shook it. "We have much to discuss and I would prefer not to do it under the rays of these suns."

President Chapman nodded. "Follow me."

The elderly man lead El-ick inside to an enormous room which contained a single table and two chairs. The President's guard remained outside, as did El-ick's own.

El-ick took a seat as Chapman did the same. The old man spoke first. "I understand your people want you for crimes of war." The statement was clearly a question in disguise.

El-ick smirked. "You might say that. I no longer share the goals of the Over-mind and feel it is my duty to change things. We must recapture the fires and values of our first days as a hybrid species if we are to survive. "

"I see," Chapman said cautiously. "You are giving up the ancient vendetta, the revenge of a dead race?"

"I am."

"Our forces are weak and in disarray. We have scattered our ships among our colonies. Many need repairs. If we give you the sanctuary you seek, we put ourselves at further risk."

"No. Your worlds would be at risk, regardless. Do you not believe the dead, as you call us, will retaliate for your actions, whether I am here? It would be foolish for you to assume they will not try to exploit your current weakness. I offer you aid in trade for shelter. I need a place where I can confront my enemy on my terms away from Earth and you... you need all the help you can get for when they come, and they will. They will come in greater force than has ever moved against your worlds at once."

"You claim you will use your ship, *Scar*, for our defense, yet we know you care about your crew."

El-ick laughed. "It will be for the greater good, will it not, President Chapman, if I defeat my enemy?"

"We would be insane to turn down your help if what you say is true. *Scar* alone is a great asset to any fleet. If you will defend this planet when the time comes, then I will grant you the sanctuary you so desperately seek. I also ask that you keep your word and hand over the woman aboard your ship and the android who accompanied her home to us."

"Agreed," El-ick concluded. "I must return to the *Scar* now. We can fine tune the terms of our agreement later. I have many things to attend to before my brethren come."

Chapter 40

GAROK

"Lord Garok," Admiral Yagsil said as his half-plastic face stared at Garok from the *Rot's* view screen. Garok hid his disgust for the man. Yagsil had suffered major, irreversible damage to his features during first interstellar combat with the colonies two years ago when his fighter had taken heavy fire from a human rail-gun. His wounds required y replacing his entire left side with synthetic material. The sight made Garok sick inside. He would have ended his own life rather than display such a blatant and disgusting appearance to his peers and superiors. Garok scowled at him and waited for the Admiral to get on with it.

"The fleet is ready, my lord," Yagsil said.

Only then did Garok smile. "Let me see it," he said.

The communications officer of *Rot* switched the screen to a panoramic view of the massive gathering of the Earth forces. Garok was happy to have Yagsil gone from his sight, but more so by the mighty armada.

There were four hulking troop ships, nine other battleships like the *Rot* herself, several clusters of destroyers, three fighter carriers, and too many smaller cruisers to count. He leaned into his command chair and let the majesty of the moment sink in. This time, the colonies would fall. The humans had no hope left with their fleet weakened and scattered among their worlds. It was a futile effort to save as many souls as they could. Best of all, though, he knew El-ick would wait for him. The *Hyperion* boarded and stolen from a space dock in Earth orbit. Only El-ick could manage a feat so cunning and insane. Indeed, it was that act which had allowed Garok to push those who supported him into action. Somewhere along the line, the ancient edict of revenge on humans at all costs had faded in importance. All he cared about, at this moment, was El-ick. The fool would meet the true death as his hands and Garok knew that, then and only then, would his position of power be secure. He turned to his helmsman. "Take us to Alpha Centauri Prime. Keep our speed to where the rest of the fleet can keep up."

The *Rot* was the most advanced in the Earth fleet. It was not as powerful or as large as the enormous monster that El-ick commanded, but the *Scar* was a "planet killer", breaking through a world's defenses and nuking it into the stone age. The *Rot* was a true ship of the line. They built her for power, but a unique power. Her systems went head-to-head with other ships in direct combat. She was fast, too. Until the *Hyperion's* return, she'd been the fastest known ship employed by either side in this war. As the stars blurred and she streaked into Leap Space, Garok smiled again, envisioning El-ick's head before him on a spike.

Chapter 41

EL-ICK

E l-ick studied the data from the long-range sensors via the screen on the arm of his command chair. He knew Garok would come in force, but this was beyond reason, even for that pompous fool. A whole two-thirds of not just Earth Fleet, but every ship controlled by the dead was less than an hour away. The humans' ragtag excuse for a fleet was gathering and preparing to leap into his sector at this very moment, but they would be too late. That meant during the initial attack, only *Griffin*, the barely repaired *Hercules*, and the exploration ship *Hyperion* would defend the world below.

On the upside, the planet, being the heart of the Human Republic, was home to a thousand or more of the small fighter craft the humans were so fond of. El-ick had demanded that the bulk of those fighters be ready. Every second and every shot was going to count in this opening round, and he wanted to make the most of what was available to him. El-ick also had one deadly trick up his sleeve. *Scar* could more than hold her own in space combat. Her hull held eighty launch tubes, each capable of firing three nukes in rapid succession. She sat among the stars with her engines primed. The second the Earth fleet leaped into the system, El-ick was going to charge them with all her guns blazing

118

right down their throats. They would target the missiles at the fleet's capital ships while *Scar* essentially rammed through the mass of small support vessels. *Scar* could take the damage and survive for a time. Her sacrifice would reduce the fleet's numbers heavily, though, and should at least put them on the defensive for minutes as they regrouped. It would be up to the *Hyperion*, under Dirk's command, and the other ships to hold the line and protect the planet below at that point. *Scar* would be in no position to do so. With Garok in command, however, the fleet would focus on the *Scar* and not the planet. No matter what Garok had told the others back on Earth, El-ick knew Garok's primary concern would be his demise.

Chapter 42

KA-JHEA

The interior of the vast underground hangar was astounding. The resources these colonies had access to must be incredible. For the moment, though, the entire place was quiet, and that was a marvel. She stood in a short line, third and last of the three fighter squadron leaders from the *Scar*. They lined a hundred and forty pilots up in ranks behind her, all clad in dull black uniforms and gleaming boots. A human officer in a pure white uniform, followed by two civilians, stood not far away. They were close enough that the officer noticed her.

He's actually pursing his lips while looking me over. The thought made her smile, despite the lack of respect. *Maybe he doesn't realize that I'm dead? Technically, anyway. Wonder if he has the chops to handle me, though?*

"I am General Hallachek, commander of all Terran Coalition Fighter Wings. For the moment, that means I am your commander as well. We are pleased to have you join us and want to assure you that the transponders installed on your fighters will prevent any friendly fire from occurring. I am attaching your first squadron to our fighter contingent to help protect the capitol ships, including your *Scar*, while the second and third squadrons attack their transport and drop ships. I have detached twenty Hipper gunships to assist your attack on the transports. We must destroy them quickly."

Hallachek paused a moment, hands on his hips. Other than a line of brass buttons on the front of his jacket and epaulets over each shoulder, his uniform was bare of decoration. A point in his favor. A holstered weapon hung from the belt around his waist. Still, he didn't stand up very well when compared to El-ick.

"Questions?" he asked at last, still looking at her.

The silence stretched out. Apparently, no one had any.

"Very good, then! Let's get to our ships and prepare. Dismissed!"

She turned and ran toward her Hades fighter.

Chapter 43

GAROK

The *Rot* led the Earth fleet into normal space. "Holy Hell!" Garok heard his helmsman screaming. The bridge erupted into chaos. A barrage of nukes was already blazing its way across the stars towards them. "El-ick!" Garok cursed. "Evasive maneuvers! Now!" Only the *Rot's* super speed engines saved it from destruction. The battleship's engines redlined as it dropped hard below the first wave of missiles. Another wave followed, hot on the heels of the first. "Counter Measures!" Garok ordered, but his weapons officer was ahead of him. The *Rot* spat interceptors at the incoming nukes as its ship-to-ship rail-guns opened us as well to thin the wave even more than a third wave bore down on it. The *Rot* took several hits before she was through the worst of the storm. "Damage report!" Garok barked. He stood up, gritting his teeth in anger as an explosion shook the *Rot* and forced him back into his command chair despite his rage.

"Minor damage, sir! Our armor is holding!" an officer shouted at him. "All major systems are still online!"

"The *Scar* is closing on us! She's approaching at ramming speed!"

What the hell? Garok stared at the massive dreadnought which filled the *Rot's* view screen. *Has El-ick gone mad?*

"Get us out of here!" Garok wailed. The *Rot's* engines gave another mighty burst of power and she darted along the underside of the *Scar*. The rail-gun spewing a trail of fire across the Dreadnought as it passed.

Garok called up a view from the aft sensors. The fleet was a mess. The *Scar's* barrage had cut it to pieces. One of the huge troop transports motionless, gutted, leaking energy from its engine into space, and beyond, the remains of many battleships filled the space where the *Scar* had torn through their lines. He couldn't even guess at the losses inflicted on the smaller vessels that the dreadnought had plowed directly into.

"Sir!" an officer shouted. "We have three human ships breaking orbit from the planet. They're moving on an intercept course."

Garok looked up at the *Rot's* main screen. The ships looked as if they were in some kind of cloud. "Magnification." he ordered. The image became clearer. "My God," he breathed. The cloud wasn't a problem with the *Rot's* sensors at all. It was a swarm of fighters the likes of which Garok had never seen before.

"Have the fleet launch all fighters. Tell them to cover the transports. I want troops on the ground as quickly as possible." Garok whirled on to face his comm officer, his eyes burning with anger and hatred. "Order every remaining capital ship to target the *Scar*. I want to see it burn in nuclear fire."

"Y-Y-Yes, sir," the comm officer stammered under the heat of his rage.

"I'm coming for you El-ick," Garok whispered. "Helmsman! Bring us around. Engage the *Scar*. All weapons, FIRE!"

Chapter 44

RON

The troops they gave him were all recruits, barely out of Basic Training. Ron found himself in command of the entire southern ground defense for the capital city of New Charlotte. In desperation, he promoted Chad to sergeant. This was a second chance. Chad lost two stripes previously because of his a volcanic temper. Ron had seen none of that, just a relaxed, hard-working guy. In the last year he worked so long with the man, that they thought alike tactically despite their differences outside of uniform. Five hundred soldiers now occupied the tiny outpost the two of them had manned on their own. If they dead dropped ferals into the desert beyond the city, the monsters were certainly going to be in for a fight if they tried to reach the city below.

Ron stood on top of the outpost's roof, scanning the night sky with his binoculars. His troops had an advantage: they'd see any pods of the ships in space launched at the planet's surface and be able to move to intercept them if necessary. Ron knew the deciding battle for the fate of Alpha Centauri was the one being fought among the stars, but it was his job to protect the civilian population down here in the sand, and it was one he took seriously. He would carry out his orders until his dying breath.

A streak of orange shot through the darkness above. He knew what it was. Falling like a meteorite, the pod crashed into the sand miles beyond the perimeter he'd established around the city. It smashed into the earth like a bomb. Even from where he stood, Ron could see the impact through his powerful binoculars. It was a tried-and-true dead tactic. The pods hit hard enough to do a world of damage and enough of the creatures would survive the impact to wreak havoc and spread the disease to the human populace. Their numbers would grow with every death, enough to make up for any loss as the pod touched down.

Ron's breath caught in his chest as a second pod appeared in the sky, then another, and another... He lost count after the fiftieth lit up the sky above. It wasn't their numbers that frightened him, though. It was the direction the pods were falling. They fell in or near New Charlotte herself. He watched as explosions from the impact of the pods rocked the great city below. Flames rose and spread through her streets and from the craters where the pods touched down, the dead flowed forth into her streets. It was unimaginable. Something was terribly wrong. The orbital defenses should have stopped any pods on a trajectory which took them into the city, but clearly that didn't happen. They must have destroyed or disabled the defenses, leaving the city vulnerable to direct attack from space. Most soldiers on the surface dug in along the perimeter under Ron's command. There was no one beyond the normal law enforcement personnel left inside New Charlotte to confront or hold back the hordes of flesh-eating monsters, which were now running amok in the city proper. Ron glanced at Chad and realized he must be thinking the same thing. "Order everyone to fall back to New Charlotte!" he yelled.

"Too late, sir. They're too close. I think we're going to have to face them."

"I think you're right, Sergeant."

Chapter 45

CLAUDIA

Admiral El-ick kept his word, and he released them, she and Frank, to the authorities of Alpha Centauri Prime as soon as the Human Republic agreed to his terms. A shuttle from the Scar had transported them to the surface. They'd been through grueling hours of questions from the government, med scans to make sure they wouldn't infect the populace of New Charlotte with the deadly virus, and finally hours addressing the world's press. Some of the reporters' questions were worse than the ones posed by the government because of their extremely personal nature. One man asked if she and Frank were sleeping together, although Frank was now a walking mass of open metal and looked every inch the android that he was. After all the hoopla with the press was over with, they assigned two soldiers to Claudia and Frank as their "personal guard" so they could go out into the city. Though valued by the leadership of the Human Republic for intel on what Earth was like now, the guards were there to monitor them.

Claudia took Frank to a diner that called itself "The Oasis in the Sand" which served many old style Earth foods. As she and Frank sat the table discussing their ordeal and their newfound freedom, the two guards waited outside the establishment on the street, monitoring them through the plexi-glass window beside their table. Claudia shoved a fork of fish that tasted like chicken into her mouth as Frank expressed his sincere apologies for the fourth time for being unable to tell her what he was during their years aboard the Hyperion. Regulations had demanded he keep his nature secret.

"I was the ace-in-the-hole versus unforeseen disasters..."

Frank stopped in mid-sentence. His pupils dilated wider. "Get down!" he screamed at her, yanking her from her chair onto the floor underneath their table with him as an explosion boomed on the street outside. Shards of glass blew inward and clattered across the top of their table. Frank stood up, knocking over the table, which had been their shield. Claudia watched him closely.

"It's safe for the moment. Our guards are dead. I suggest we secure the weapons they carried and seek a place of shelter."

Claudia got to her feet, staring out into the street beyond. Fires were burning in the shattered remains of several buildings. Roughly a block away, a massive metal sphere was halfway buried in the ground. "Is that what hit us?" she asked Frank.

"I believe so," Frank confirmed. "I believe nothing detonated, or we would no longer exist."

"Uh, Frank... I don't think it's a bomb."

The top of the sphere burst open and dozens upon dozens of rotting, bleeding monsters emerged from it. They poured out of it like a swarm of ants from a hive. Their howls of hunger and rage filled the night.

Frank took her arm. "We must go now, Claudia," he said and shoved her towards the restaurant's entrance. "Run!"

A dead man from the pod spotted them and shook his head wildly, slinging saliva and blood through the air as he howled at them and came after them at a sprint.

Frank snatched the rifle from the cooked and broken body of a guard and opened fire at the man. The rifle's bullets traced a line from his stomach to his head as Frank found his aim. The last round blew the man's head apart like it was an overripe melon, and the decaying form crumpled to the street with a thud. Eight more of the things took his place, charging at them as Frank told her to run again, lowering his rifle and following her, as she spun on her heels and took off with her legs pumping as hard as they could.

They rounded the corner and came face to face with a speeding hover car heading towards them. Frank shoved Claudia from its path but didn't have time to dodge himself. It slammed into him like an old Earth train, tossing him through the air into the window of a nearby shop. The car spun out of control and vanished around the corner. Claudia scrambled to her feet. "Frank!"

Frank emerged from the shop, stumbling towards her. He held his metal arm folded over his stomach area. Claudia raced to him. "Are you ok?"

It took him a moment to notice she was there.

"I have internal damage to my internal systems, including my power supply."

He removed the hand covering his stomach and Claudia saw a large dent from the impact with the car and a laceration leaking a black oil-like fluid and something that looked like blood. Was it real or synthetic? "I'm afraid I've lost our only weapon, and this may prove rather a problem."

He smiled, but looked nothing like the Frank she knew.

"Can you run?" she asked.

"Yes. However, at my current rate of power leakage, there're only hours until I shutdown completely."

Claudia wondered if Frank could die. Would he cease to exist if he shut down, or would his mind lay dormant in something akin to human sleep?

"Come on, Frank!" she said, and helped him up.

A pack of howling, dead creatures came sprinting around the corner of the road at them.

Chapter 46

KA-JHEA

There was a thin sheen of sweat at her temples and her upper lip as her flight of fighters and gunships finally broke through the atmosphere of New Charlotte and into true space. Sometimes her body was still trying to reject the alien presence that now maintained it, while at other times, it reached a happy medium. Sweating was a welcome, normal procedure for cooling that she embraced and was grateful for. It was also a reminder that she was under stress and needed to be careful.

Her collection of forty some-odd fighters and five gunships were rapidly approaching one of the already orbiting troopships. Any moment now, she knew, the first rank of pods ranked upon the colossal ship would drop, like overripe fruit from a tree. *We need to destroy them before that happens. Catch 'em still on vine, so to speak.*

There was no sign of protective fighters as she streaked in, already lining up for her first run. She flicked the safety off on her guns and slid her fingers around the dual triggers.

"Good hunting, and look out for each other. See you on the other side."

There were one or two grunts in reply, but nothing to show that any of them cared whether she lived or died.

130

Concentrate, take deep breaths. The target wavered. Sweat rolled into her right eye. The release mechanism for an entire row of pods lay exposed and surrounded by the targeting cue. She pressed down on the triggers, hosing the machinery in a hail of explosive, uranium-tipped rounds. Before her, a brief, but enveloping flare of light obscured her view.

The troop ship was still there, but it looked like one entire row of pods was stuck. Right behind her, the rest of her ships followed, launching missiles and firing their own guns.

Several defensive guns opened up, and three of her comrades more or less vanished when the heavy bore guns scored hits on their ships. One of the Hipper gunships got caught in a cross-fire from two different defensive batteries and came apart in a white-hot cloud of molten debris.

She circled around for another run, concentrating again, trying to aim, flinching each time a piece of wreckage buffeted her ship.

Chapter 47

RON

The mingled rays of the two suns had just touched the horizon. The smell of rot, spilled bowels, and vomit was heavy in his nose.

"Duck!" Chad yelled, and Ron threw himself flat on the sand.

Chad cut loose with an extended burst from the grenade launcher. He tracked from left to right, each grenade tossing bodies in the air, shredding and slashing the onrushing horde, but not slowing it.

Ron glanced at the man beside him: one of the green recruits. He hadn't wanted to leave the boy behind. Boy was correct. He couldn't be over fifteen. Fifteen, but wearing the uniform of a soldier. Someone or something shot him. The wound was high on his back, just about centered between his shoulder blades, but no exit wound on the other side.

Right now, a bloody froth was draining from between the boy's clenched teeth. Sand clung to his face and neck.

The howls rose and grew closer. The grenade launcher fell silent. "I'm out, sir!" screamed Chad. "Everyone else is dead."

Ron climbed to his knees, ready to lift the boy back over his shoulder. He gagged, finding himself nearly face to face—The boy's eyes were open, opaque, filmed over and blinking. *He passed over!*

Ron threw himself backwards, crabbing away, even as the thing stirred into motion, following him. Both climbed to their feet, and the now feral boy leaped at him, hands outstretched. Ron stepped to the left and threw a right cross at the kid's jaw. Terrible pain exploded from the impact of his hand. Might have broken a knuckle.

The undead thing dropped to a knee, and Ron didn't hesitate to draw his combat knife and stab. The blade's point went into its eye to the hilt. He tried to yank it free as it fell over, but the handle slipped through his fingers. The newly dead, or dead again, body slid to the ground.

"Run, Captain!" shouted Chad. "There's a convoy in route to us, a mile north of that hill. Heard a lot of shooting and explosions, but maybe we'll find help."

Ron looked at the Chad's face, "Okay, Chad, lead on!"

Chapter 48

EL-ICK

"The Forward armor's compromised in many locations!" A bridge crewman shouted.

Sparks flew all around El-ick, sitting in his command chair.

"All nukes spent!" his weapons officer informed him.

"We're taking heavy fire to port, sir! *Rot* is making another strafing run!"

"The other ships?" El-ick asked, calm amid the chaos.

"The remaining four battleships of the fleet are closing behind us! The aft armor is failing in sections. We have hull breaches on all sides!"

El-ick smiled in the dim light of the bridge. *Scar* could take damage. Its massive size rendered it hard to destroy, and, with luck, no major systems would fail.

"Target the *Rot*. Bring all rail-guns within range to bear on her," he ordered.

"Sir?" the weapons officer asked. "What about the other battle-ships?"

"Now," El-ick said. His tone left no room for disagreement.

Rot was the real threat to the ship with advanced systems and speed that countered *Scar's* mass.

The *Scar's* hull took major damage from the impacts of the hundreds of smaller vessels it plowed through moments before. If Garok figured out what to exploit, they were in very real trouble.

Another barrage of combined fire from the closing battleships struck the *Scar*.

The communications station to El-ick's left exploded, sending its operator rolling across the floor in flames. The crew hadn't faced this level of damage or threat before. She'd been a juggernaut since she'd first left the space dock. El-ick was proud of the way they were almost single-handedly tackling the entire Earth fleet by themselves.

The *Scar's* entire port battery of rail-guns fired at the Rot. The sleek battleship dodged most of the fire, but took several hits.

El-ick knew Garok would not make a suicide run against him. He was a coward and greedy for the spoils he'd gain upon El-ick's death. Yet such a threat existed from the other ships under his command. With the *Scar's* limited array of weapons at its disposal, El-ick doubted he could fend off such an attack if Garok ordered it. El-ick shifted in his chair. "What is the status of the planet?"

"The troop transport has launched hundreds of pods into the atmosphere, despite our fighters' attempts to stop them. The *Hyperion* and the other ships have prevented the remaining destroyers and cruisers from getting orbital barrage positions, however."

El-ick weighed his options as the *Rot* darted by the *Scar* again, this time flying over her and unleashing a stream of nukes directly into her top side: Continuous explosions, impacts felt on the bridge. As *Rot* streaked away, The *Scar's* rail-guns fire chased after her and scored a well-placed hit. *Rot* lurched too hard to starboard as one of her three aft engines blew in an eruption of flame and radiation before flickering out. She floundered in space for a moment, taking fire from *Scar*, before she righted herself and began a new series of evasive maneuvers which allowed her to escape the pounding she was taking.

At her best, the Scar—but she isn't at her best...far from it. We approach the end. No missiles remained, and she had taken a great deal of damage. "Bring us about," El-ick ordered his helmsman. "Give the general order to abandon ship."

"Sir?" his communications officer asked, looking as if he surely must have heard El-ick wrong.

"Give the order to abandon ship. No more of this crew will die fighting my battle for me. Garok is my responsibility alone."

The look in El-ick's eyes was hard and cold as he watched the officer at the comm station activate the abandon ship protocols. El-ick turned to his the bridge's engineering officer. "Route all systems to my control," he said, taping some keys on the arm of his command chair.

Klaxons blared throughout the *Scar* as its crew raced for the shuttles in the massive ship's hangar bays and spherical escape pods were jettisoned into space from every level of the ship. El-ick switched the *Scar's* rail-guns into a defensive mode, covering the vessels of his fleeing crew. Somewhere aboard the *Rot*, he imagined Garok wondering what in the devil he was up to. A smile split his full lips as he watched the *Rot* coming around at *Scar* once more. Few in Earth Command knew the true extent of the *Scar's* maneuverability. While she was certainly no match for a ship like the *Rot*, she was insanely quick for a ship her size. The *Rot* swooped in, El-ick keyed a command into the re-routed helm controls. *Scar* lurched as all her engines fired at once and took her directly into the *Rot's* path. *Rot* smashed into the forward side of the *Scar*. Her speed drove her into the *Scar* like a needle before exploding, taking a good fourth of the *Scar* with her. El-ick felt the coldness of space leaking onto the surrounding bridge. The *Scar's* internal light atmosphere vented to space. It was only a matter of minutes until the residual heat was gone as well and he froze solid where he sat. He checked the status of the weapon systems. Forty percent of the *Scar's* rail-guns were still functional, although with the crew gone, the ammo would last seconds. The remaining four battleships stood off. They'd even ceased firing as if too stunned to take action. El-ick cursed as his continued systems check revealed the *Scar's* engines were off line. He was a sitting duck and unable to take the fight to them. He had only one option left. El-ick punched in a series of commands and the *Scar's* rail-guns emptied their remaining ammo at the battleships. They all took several hits. It was just enough to stir their captains to anger once more, El-ick hoped. Their engines flared and the streaked toward the *Scar* with all guns blazing. The impacts of missiles blowing large chunks from the *Scar's* battered remains and the constant stream of rail-gun fire punching holes through the remnants of its armor filled El-ick with a sense of rapture. The sounds of destruction were a symphony to him. Ice had formed over parts of his body and his legs frozen solid. His hand snapped and popped with the noise of breaking tendons and tearing muscles as he lifted it just enough to hit the last key needed to start the pre-programmed sequence he'd prepared. As his finger stabbed the button, he tried to laugh, but there was no air. A fitting end to life he couldn't remember before the virus. His dreams were large though: memories of glorious starship battles; ground combat; slaughter; and taking no prisoners. He wondered where it all came from. He was just a colonist, wasn't he, in that previous life? No time to wonder...

Scar exploded like a supernova as the battleships closed in on it. The blast vaporized two. The next closest took heavy damage and the final battleship spun like a top into the void, struggling to right itself as the concussive wave of the blast pushed on.

Chapter 49

PETER

P eter stood at the engineering station on the bridge of the *Hyperion* behind the command chair. He watched the events unfolding on the view screen over Dirk's shoulder. The darkness of space was lit by a massive explosion as the *Scar* blew itself to pieces, taking most of the remaining enemy capital ships with it. Dirk was screaming orders, and the bridge was in a state of chaos. The Hyperion was being swarmed by Hades' fighters. The small craft flew all around it, blasting holes in its armor as the *Hyperion's* rail-guns blazed away in continuous streams of shifting fire trying to fend them off.

Peter knew they had the advantage now. The enemy's cruisers and few remaining destroyers were no match for them. A cheer rose as several groups of human fighters swooped in, driving off the bulk of the swarm attacking the ship. Of course, he knew too that the greatest threat left from the dead were the hulking troop transports which continued to launch shock troop pods at the planet below.

"We have to take out those transports!" Dirk raged. "Maximum speed!"

The helmsman closed the distance between *Hyperion* and the closest transport. The *Hyperion* did sport super heavy armor, and

138

that was the main thing that kept her alive during the battle which raged around her.

"Peter, weapons status?" Dirk asked.

"She's down to her last eight nukes," Peter answered.

"Then we better make them count. Launch six at that transport as soon as you get a clear shot!"

Six missiles trailing fire spat from the *Hyperion's* forward tubes. Not a single one reached their target. A wave of Hades fighters came out of nowhere, intercepting the attack. A group of fighters from the *Scar* quickly met and engaged them.

"One more shot!" Peter warned.

"No!" Dirk shook his head. "Two nukes won't do it. I need options."

Peter knew the *Hyperion* better than anyone else, living or dead. Now, he had to save the day. He wasn't a hero or even a warrior despite his newly gained post death training. He was an engineer and would always be. Peter searched and found nothing that would do the job. Then it hit him. He smiled and looked Dirk in the eye. "I have a plan, but it's risky. It will endanger this ship and everyone aboard."

"Let's do it," Dirk replied.

"Rerouting helm controls to the engineering station. I'm going to need to put us next to that transport."

Dirk shot him a look that told him to get on it with it. The look quickly became one of fear as he watched Peter steer the Hyperion into a docking position as it approached the transport.

If the troop carrier had been better armed, they would've blown to space dust as Peter brought the hull of the *Hyperion* within inches of the transport's hull. Peter channeled every ounce of power left into the *Hyperion's* Leap drive and activated it. When a ship emerged from Leap space, it created a close, small scale explosion. Peter was counting on the reverse happening here, and in theory, it was possible. A Leap bubble formed around the ship, slicing through the armored hull of the transport and sucking large chunks of the vessel into Leap space along with the *Hyperion*. Peter imagined he could hear the screech of the metal tearing before the Hyperion leaped away and the transport exploded milliseconds after the Hyperion vanished.

Hyperion dropped out Leap space a suitable distance away from the battle but still close enough to be within visual range of it. He glimpsed what was happening around Alpha Centauri before the cracked view screen went black. The other battleships fought the last of their fighters and small cruisers trying to flee.

The *Hyperion* was in rough shape, power reserves drained and she drifted lifelessly among the stars amid the debris she'd carried with her. Systems shorted out on the bridge as the backwash of the leap caught up with them. No ship pulled another into Leap space with them and doing so had cost them. He watched as the bridge's ceiling buckled and gave way to the stress of the re-entry. A jagged piece of metal flew from the exploding helm controls and planted itself directly in Dirk's forehead. The captain slumped forward in the chair as the true death claimed him.

Peter took over, barking orders, as he raced to stir the rest of the crew into action. He tied what was left of the ship's internal sensors into the controls of the engineering station and coordinated the damage control teams being hastily assembled throughout the ship.

"Are you taking over command?" asked a voice over his shoulder.

Peter turned in the chair.

He was a short, slim guy who always took Dirk's orders without comment or question. Half of the man's face was beet red, like a bad sunburn. A moment later, recognition came. "You are the helmsman."

"Yes, I am Hatron, helmsman and second officer."

"What did you want to ask me?"

"Whether you were taking over command."

Peter hesitated, looking around the bridge area. Several crewmen stood or sat at their posts, all apparently waiting for his answer.

"Yes, I am."

Hatron nodded. "Very good, sir. What are your orders?"

Chapter 50

CLAUDIA

C laudia raced through the streets of New Charlotte with Frank at her side. They'd been on the run for a while now and the exertion was taking its toll on Frank. The android was moving more slowly and his level of lucidity seemed to come and go.

Sometimes he would babble to himself as they ran, chanting a series of numbers that sounded like some sort of binary code. Claudia knew the leak in his power cell was shutting him down and all the energy spent staying on the move was only making it worse. They couldn't stop, though, not if they wanted to stay alive. The dead were everywhere. Everyone they killed got up and joined their ranks, causing their numbers to grow at an exponential rate.

Claudia kept up her frantic pace, trying to find somewhere, anywhere, safe. Her breath came in gasps as she pushed herself on. People were screaming over the howls of the feral dead. They dragged a man to her right from a store through its front window. There were three of the creatures tearing at him and trying to pull him apart so that they could share his flesh. To her left, a naked man with horrific wounds to his chest, that no longer bled, sat on his haunches, gnawing on the arm of a beautiful woman in an evening gown who lay at his feet. The woman was still alive, but unmoving. Her wet eyes met Claudia's in a silent plea as tears streamed down her cheeks.

Claudia turned her eyes away.

"Look out!" she heard Frank yell at her. She barely flung herself to the side as a man with a massive hole in his chest and smeared with blood leaped out from an alleyway as they passed it. Claudia lost her balance and fell to the ground. Frank grabbed him, lifting him into the air with a single hand, and slammed him so hard into the metal wall of the building beside them she heard the man's bones snap like twigs. Frank tossed the man aside and offered Claudia a hand up. She took it, noticing that one of Frank's eyes had gone dark as he pulled her to her feet. She asked him about it, but he cut her off. "That large warehouse it is our closest hope of secure shelter," he informed her.

Together, they sprang forward again. Claudia's heart pounded in her chest as they covered the remaining distance to it. Claudia tried the building's immense doors, but they wouldn't open.

"Step aside," Frank ordered her. An interface device popped out of his wrist like the blade of a switchblade. He plunged it into the control panel beside the door and his good eye closed as if he were no longer inside the metal form which stood beside her. A moment later, Frank opened his eye at the same time the door slid inward, allowing them entrance. As soon as they were inside, it closed behind them. There were no lights. The interior of the warehouse was as dark as a cloudy and starless night.

"What is this place?" Claudia asked.

"It is a storage facility currently owned by the Earth's historical preservation society according to what I could learn from the computer. Come on!" Frank said, darting off into the shadows, his heavy feet clanging on the metal of the floor. "I believe I have found our means of escape."

Without warning, one of the servo motors in his left leg stopped functioning and Claudia watched him fall, skidding across the floor to come to rest a few feet from the large tarp covered object he'd been leading her towards. "Frank!" she cried out and rushed to him. She leaned over him as he looked up at her with eyes that were now totally dark. "This is where I leave you, Claudia." His voice was weak and slurred.

"No, Frank. There's gotta to be something in here we can use to repair you. Jury rig an alternative power source."

With a visible effort, the android shook his head. "If the warehouse's data files are correct, the key should be in something referred to as the "glove box". God speed, Claudia Coyne."

Frank's head dropped to the floor and his body lay motionless.

"Damn you, Frank," she cursed through her tears. She stood and jerked the tarp off the vehicle it covered. She couldn't help but laugh as she saw the brilliant red chrome of the car's hood. If she remembered her old Earth history correctly, this sort of model was called a Barchetta. There wasn't a door, so she hopped inside. Her eyes scanned the car's interior, looking for a box, but didn't see one. Finally, she noticed a small closed compartment in front of the passenger seat. Inside were the keys, just like Frank had told her. She stuck them in the ignition and the engine roared to life. Revving it a few times to make sure it worked, she floored the gas. The tires spun out, squealing, as the car hurled itself towards the door they'd entered through. It slid open as she approached and knew it doing so was Frank's work. He must have pre-programmed it to be ready for their means of escape. The Barchetta bounced into the street. Claudia swerved to avoid a pack of creatures charging towards her, jerking the wheel hard to the left. She righted the car, narrowly avoiding crashing into a restaurant at the edge of the road. Wind blew through her hair as she picked up speed and drove onward towards the edge of New

Charlotte and the desert beyond. Getting out of the city was the major priority. If she survived doing that, she'd figure out what came next later.

The airport isn't too far from here. Just follow the road.

Chapter 51

RON

The sky was gray. In the last hour, the wind picked up, bringing with it towering storm clouds, but no relief from the heat of the twin suns overhead.

Ron paused and leaned over, his breathing ragged and uneven.

Most of the re-supply column was burning. Only two vehicles out of twenty were still intact. Thousands of bodies littered the cratered ground surrounding the road. In a near hopeless last stand, the officer commanding the column had called down an artillery strike on the position. Too late to save anyone, though. Everyone died.

"These MACs are great," said Chad, referring to the tracked tank-like vehicle he was sitting in. MAC was short for Mobile Armored Carrier.

Ron didn't reply. He hefted the heavy box of ammunition onto his shoulder and handed it up to the man sitting up in the turret. "That's eight boxes," said Chad, lowering the box onto the tray beside him. "I just need to link this one up and feed it into the well, and we're ready." He patted the 30mm cannon barrel. "We'll be packing quite a wallop with this baby on full-auto, sir."

"Good," Ron answered, grabbing his Assault Multi-Purpose, or AMP, rifle from where it leaned against the vehicle. Someone was approaching.

A haggard-looking sergeant limped over to the two men. On his left arm was the brassard of the military police. "I'm Sergeant-Major Rudd and I've got four men left. Can we hitch a ride, sir?"

"That's up to you, Sergeant-Major. We're heading back to the capitol. Sure could use your help."

The Sergeant-Major turned around and made a waving motion with his right hand. Four shapes rose from the ground and ran towards them.

"Where'd you guys come from, sir?" Rudd asked.

"We can from Sarhaggen Point, the outpost over-looking the desert."

Rudd looked shocked. "Just you and him, sir? That's ten miles from here."

"There may be other survivors, but my men were green, Sergeant! Most died in the second wave of attacks we faced."

Rudd's face went stony, and he raised his AMP rifle, centering it on Ron's chest. "You a deserter, Captain?"

"What if we both are, Sergeant?" asked Chad from his perch up in the MAC's turret. He held a pistol aimed at the military policeman.

"Guess we'd have a problem then, Sergeant."

"And if we aren't deserters?" Ron asked, watching the man swallow.

"Well, sir, we really have no proof of you doing anything but your duty. I'd like to apologize for jumping to conclusions."

"What do you say to that, Sergeant Morris?" Ron asked Chad. "Think he's sincere?"

Chad grinned. "You told him earlier that we needed help, sir. I'd say let them pile into the back of the MAC and let's go. People are dying as we speak."

"Pile in then, Sergeant, and we'll get out of here."

The man gave a shaky grin in return and then followed his men through the hatch in the back.

Taking a chance on that one. But was there a choice, anyway?

Chapter 52

REAPER

From above, the scale of the buildings and the light monorail that linked the entire complex of Braxton Airport to the capital of New Charlotte was quite impressive. Reaper did his best to memorize all he could until the moment the shuttles set down.

The survivors from the Scar all landed in mass on the tarmac of the civilian spaceport two kilometers from the capitol's environs. Reaper's marines formed a perimeter, and even now were engaging ferals. The crew armed themselves, but lacked training for this type of combat. Better to get them into a secure building and use the marines for anything else.

"Most of the capitol is burning, sir," said one of his grizzled veterans. He couldn't remember the man's name at the moment, but noticed that the man was hunchbacked and missing an ear.

"Gather a squad and we'll clear the terminal building. Might use that monorail to ferry survivors out of the city. Otherwise, we'll be fighting our own kind for a long time."

"Right away, sir," the man replied and turned away.

Reaper took a moment to check his rifle over, and to test draw his knife a few times. No telling when or where he would need to use a blade, but it was well-used.

He walked towards the terminal. It looked like a fragile piece of human confectionary, all airy spaces, glass and ribbon-thin steel supports, but he knew it could withstand more punishment. Small arms weren't a threat.

On the inside, he could see that many refugees must have sought shelter here. The problem was no one to protect them. Somehow, the ferals got inside. Blood smeared many of the windows. Violated, eviscerated bodies lay sprawled everywhere inside. Most weren't moving.

He wanted to feel something, but the most he could muster was a dim memory of his own near blind bloodlust. Only the combat itself engaged him now. Slaughter and feasting were for the ferals.

For the mindless killing machines.

The nameless veteran came up behind him, followed by nine more marines.

"We'll go in right here, at the main entrance. Take point," Reaper said, pointing at the veteran.

The man nodded and stepped through the shattered doors. He held his weapon ready. Ferals weren't the only worry. Snipers and other types of specialist soldier often complemented their mass attack style.

The rest of the squad followed, with Reaper walking in the middle. They entered a cavernous lobby. At the far side were ticket counters and concourses branching off to the various terminal buildings. Amid all this, the slaughter was still underway.

Reaper's men fired, taking out each feral using as few rounds as possible.

Bodies rose all around them, some half-eaten, while others wore the mottled-pattern desert camouflage he was used to associating with his own side.

Moments later, the lobby was quiet. Reaper's men paused a moment to re-load, then when they were ready, he dispatched them in pairs , to clear each area.

Somehow, when they were all dispatched, the hunchbacked soldier was still there with him. "Come with me. We'll take the tower."

They came to a service door marked "Authorized Personnel Only."

"This is the way, sir," the man said, and tried the door.

It was unlocked and opened inwards. They entered a long passageway.

"What's your name, soldier?" Reaper asked.

"Most people call me Hunch, sir."

"Do you remember your real name?"

The man turned back toward Reaper and stared. "What does it matter?" he snapped. "I'm a good soldier and follow orders, don't I?"

"Better tone it down, or I'll rip your head off."

"I was a scientist, sir, doing important work, not a soulless, undead killer. I lived, loved, and lost. Your people took my only reasons for living and turned me into this...this thing that craves the most hideous things."

"You remember." Reaper's voice was soft.

"My name was Norman Botts, sir."

Reaper looked at the man. "Well, Norman, we get each other through this, and I'll see what I can do to get you back to your work. We are forging something new here with our enemies."

For a moment or two longer, Botts looked him in the eye. "It's too late, sir, but it was a nice offer. We need to clear this building now before it is too late to save anyone."

They were mere steps from the end of the passage. Botts turned away and reached for the door. Reaper noticed a high-heeled shoe in the corner, against the wall.

The door opened, and a horde of ferals poured out. Botts didn't scream, but he made a mewling sound as one of them shoved a hand into his mouth. Another leaned in and bit into his throat. The weight of the bodies bore Botts backward and knocked him down. The ferals poured over him and some were already trying to get to Reaper.

He opened fire, emptying a full magazine of fifty explosive bullets into the mass of flesh, then he pulled a grenade off his harness. While backpedaling, he removed the pin, counted to three, and tossed it. The concussion blew out his eardrums and tossed him to the ground. Grisly fragments showered down on him.

While lying on his back, he licked at the blood on his lips. Nothing moved while he lay there. Nothing reacted as he got to his feet, either. He could see Botts' face beneath a tangle of charred limbs and torsos. There was a peaceful quality there now.

Wonder if I'll look like that someday?

Reaper re-loaded his rifle, slung it over his back and pulled his knife. The blade was almost 12 cm long and was double-edged. He stepped on the bodies and crossed into the stairwell beyond.

Just need to finish the job now.

Chapter 53

PETER

"We are on course for the last two transports, sir," said Hatron. "We have little more than our small caliber anti-fighter emplacements to attack with."

"Thank you, Hatron," Peter said, feeling awkward. The man needed a rank.

"Do you have a rank?"

"I am Lieutenant, sir."

"Very good. It looks like our forces are already attacking the transports, lieutenant."

"They are. That is Ka-Jhea's squadron, sir."

Ka-Jhea. I have heard of her, but can't remember seeing her. Just a name. With Claudia, he could still feel, or at least remember, something of what it felt like to love, to feel the blood move in your veins.

He remembered their last encounter in the Virtual World. *Never really made up for that. Too proud. Too eager to prove that I didn't need anyone. The sex was wonderful. Even she would admit that. Just that damn Frank that ruined it. Wonder if either of them made it? My curiosity won't let me be at peace.*

I have to know.

"We do what we can here, Lieutenant, then we see about New Charlotte."

"Yes, sir."

The two immense ships came into view on the primary display. A cloud of fighters surrounded the transports as the second one launched pods. On a secondary display off to his right, Peter watched as the anti-fighter guns opened fire on the pods. Each gun was dual-barreled and capable of 'lock-in' fire. This meant that the guns could track and attempt to second guess what the pilot would do. Vindication for bringing them into play was immediate as several pods exploded, scattering bodies and debris over a wide area.

Peter spotted a single Hades fighter braving the gauntlet of fire and debris. The fighter juked to the side, narrowly avoiding the transport's defensive fire, and launched a torpedo.

Peter said a prayer.

Chapter 54

CLAUDIA

The car literally flew across the desert. The small windshield kept her eyes squinted, but the wind, the speed and the heat all were a potent medicine for melancholy.

She almost by-passed the turnoff for the spaceport, but forced herself to slow down and take the turn. There were immediate signs that this might not have been the best idea, but she was stubborn. The remains of a pod lay less than a hundred yards to the right of the road, but the only signs of life she saw were a pair of vultures circling the wreck.

A slow but loud rumble of thunder crashed somewhere overhead. No rain or lightning. She rounded a corner, and the spaceport was there. Small spacecraft were everywhere, most of them of the same make, military shuttles painted black with a streak of red. *The Scar! They must have sent help down!*

As she drew closer, the sound of explosions and gunfire reached her. In the distance, an entire hanger exploded, sending a roiling cloud of oily smoke skyward.

With no proper plan, she allowed the car to drift to a stop near one shuttle.

A moment later, marines from the *Scar* surrounded her car.

"Please exit the vehicle."

She got out.

Chapter 55

KA-JHEA

*F*uel's almost gone. The thought meant next to nothing. Just a statistic. Might have enough for one last try.

All around her, her companions were being destroyed. Few would escape this attack, but if they failed, then escaping wasn't possible, anyway. The torpedoes the Hades fighters always carried but seldom used as the range was so short; they were close to a suicide weapon. To get close enough took nerves of steel and a lot of luck.

She apparently had both.

Her first torpedo went right in to one of the armored exhausts of the already damaged transport, with more than half of its pods still attached.

Ka-Jhea banked sharply up, out and away to the port side of the ship just as the second torpedo struck and exploded deep within the ship's engine. Suddenly, there was no coherent shape that could be called a ship, just three separate parts all disintegrating rapidly as they fell into the planet's atmosphere.

The fourth and last transport engaged its drive and warped out, fully loaded.

Success!

She felt herself relax. Her fuel gauge beeped, and moments later her engine died. Four or five other Hades fighters were drifting with her.

I'm going to die the true death, but we succeeded! So much sacrifice, but hopefully it will be worth it.

"Attention surviving fighters from the *Scar*," said the voice over her radio, "the *Hyperion* will take you aboard shortly. Just hang in there!"

She looked over her shoulder. The *Hyperion* was there.

Chapter 56

RON

The gun fired a quick burst upward and pieces of the falling pod exploded like a firework rocket. A thousand glittering fiery little pieces plunged toward the ground, trailing smoke and sparks.

"Beautiful," muttered Chad. "each one of those bastards is just a meat bomb."

He spun the turret twenty degrees to the right, engaged the target-lock, and fired another brief burst of needle-pointed rounds into the sky. Another boom and expanding cloud marked the destruction of a second pod.

"Keep it up, soldier," said Ron. In the last few minutes, the Sergeant-Major and his men disappeared. *No sense trying to tell Chad. They had a job to finish. Ironic that the other man truly deserted while they were battling the enemy.*

Chad got two more in the next five minutes, but then nothing. *Maybe the assault was over. Just mop up the survivors and go home.* Ron walked around to the back of the MAC. Both doors were open. The rear area of the MAC comprised two benches for soldiers to sit on or stand on as they rode. Nobody was there.

"The other guys bugged out, didn't they, sir?"

"Yeah. Not sure when."

159

Ron closed the doors and locked them.

"I can hear more ferals, sir. Sounds like thousands of 'em howling."

"Yeah, get us out of here and head for the airport!"

"Yes, sir!"

Ron heard several weapons fire. It was ragged fire, not disciplined. Someone was panicking. He had an idea who.

A doorway linked the rear compartment with both the turret above and the driver's compartment. He climbed through and hoisted himself up into the driver's seat. Pushed the ignition button. Various systems came online as the engine rumbled to life. There were readouts for engine status, fuel and even the ammo for the auto-cannon. Looked like they were down to roughly two hundred rounds for the cannon, and a third tank of fuel. They could reach the airport, no problem, but they wouldn't be shooting many more ferals. He grasped the joysticks, one for each hand, pushed each handle forward, and stepped on the fuel pedal.

The MAC lurched into motion. He made a looping turn by keeping the left handle forward and the right pulled back and they were heading for the airport and, coincidently, the direction they'd heard the gunfire come from.

They rounded a large rock protruding from the sand, and there they were: three survivors running frantically toward them, followed by a horde of the monsters. *The MPs...*

"Mother of God," he heard Chad murmur. "What do we do, sir?"

Ron clenched his teeth. One order, and Chad could probably drop enough of the ferals for the three deserters to reach the MAC and climb aboard. He watched the first, closest man fall, whether from a twisted ankle, or what he didn't know. The other two men ran right past him. Neither had their guns anymore. The ferals were closing in on all three. *A few seconds more and none of them would make it.*

Ron waited a few seconds more.

The horde reached the fallen man, then the next two.

The feast began.

Ron pulled the left joystick back, the right forward, and hit the gas. They made a wide, loping turn around the horde and, on the far side, found a dirt track. They turned onto it and followed it all the way to the airport.

Chapter 57

PETER

H e exited the shuttle, followed by Hatron and the pilot, Ka-Jhea. A few drops of rain fell, mixed in with the grit already blowing in the wind. A small group of people awaited him near the control tower and the huge terminal building complex. He noticed a couple of vehicles, one a small tracked military vehicle and the other an ancient ground car painted bright red.

Among the people, a woman, with blonde hair. *Claudia! Vestiges of his human response remained, or maybe he just imagined his blood racing and his heart giving an irregular thump.*

He ran across the tarmac shouting her name, as close to alive as he'd ever been once.

Something was wrong.

She wasn't running toward him. If anything, she was shrinking away.

I'm a monster now, he thought.

He slowed to a walk. Noticed the other people waiting, Reaper and a couple of human soldiers, one of them a captain.

"Captain Hoyle, I presume," said the human officer. "I am Captain Ron Davis."

"Nice to meet you, Captain," Peter heard himself answer.

All was ashes now. Claudia was crying, but making no effort to come to him.

Someone touched his elbow. The pilot Ka-Jhea. "Be strong, Captain," she whispered.

The human, Davis, was looking him over. Somehow, Peter kept a straight face.

"What can I do for you, Captain Davis?" Peter asked.

Davis smiled. "I was going to ask you the same thing. It appears you are in charge, sir. A naval captain far outranks an army captain. Our president and the entire government didn't make it out of New Charlotte."

Peter made himself stand still, fighting the trembling in his legs.

"You are in charge, sir. What are your orders?"

Peter turned, looking out over the barren dunes. Alpha Centauri Prime was truly a desolate place.

Dead as my heart.

"Gather the troops. We have a capitol to take back."

Chapter 58

Sneak Peek at Undead in Vegas

D awn is breaking on an ugly day in May when I run into heavy traffic. I'm hung over, and the inside of my truck cab smells like the Italian Sub I ate last night. High time to air things out and roll down my windows for a few minutes. Reminds me that there's a terrible story behind me, but I'll save you the details. The bare bones of my past are that I'm fifty-two, about forty pounds overweight, and sometimes need a little medicinal help after being in a loveless marriage for years.

So, where does this leave me, you might ask? On the road. In the months following my divorce, I went to a truck driving school to get a Commercial Driver's license. Been driving a company rig on my own for a month and a half now.

At the moment, I'm almost at my destination. Seen some crazy traffic the last few hours, and I'm wondering what's going on. My in-dash radio quit working, and I don't have a CB. The low man gets the beat-up piece of junk, I guess. Cheap bastard owner. I could check my cell phone, but I'm focusing on driving. I see the exit sign, then an overturned car, a police cruiser, and a bunch of cars piled together just as I take an exit ramp off Interstate

15 for Las Vegas. See an oil slick covering the road, try to slow down, clip the rear of another semi-trailer and run up and over the police cruiser. My rig careens across two lanes, overturns onto the driver's side and slides into the guardrail. I'm thrown around like a doll, but my seat belt saves me.

My heart's pounding and hands tremble as I unfasten my seat belt and climb up and out of the cab, through the passenger side. The truck's on fire, so I jump off and down to the road. People are running around, screaming and shouting for help. Someone in a Hummer drives through the crowd without stopping, and several people get run over. Something explodes not far away, and I duck the bark of a large caliber revolver. I spot a cop holding a gun. She's struggling with two people and losing the fight. I hear her scream and run her way. I have to do something. Her gun skitters across the pavement toward me. One attacker rips out her throat with his teeth, while the other gnaws an arm.

What the fuck?

I might be in zombie hell.

Smoke billows across the road, probably from my truck, and a hulking man with an axe runs through it. I scoop up the revolver and watch as the crazy guy chops both of the cannibals... and the cop!

The axe-man's face is covered with gore. His hair is stringy with sweat, and plastered to his forehead. While the bodies are still twitching, he wipes his face with a shirt sleeve, then cleans the axe blade off on the cop's pant leg. I see him squint over at me, teeth bared in a grimace as he hefts the axe.

I raise the gun, guessing five bullets left, because I only heard one shot, but who knows what I've missed already?

"Yahhhhh!" the axe-maniac screams.

I squeeze the trigger, and the gun belches fire and thunder. I miss at less than ten feet with my first shot. The guy doesn't even blink or break stride as he raises the axe on high.

My second shot hits him in the gut and ruins his day. His legs give out and crumple beneath him. My ears are ringing, and I can barely hear his screams.

He curls up into a fetal position, bleeding out between his fingers, as I leave him lying there. I make my way down the exit ramp. I stop beside a car at the edge of a parking lot.

With a large percussive thump, my tanker truck blows up and strews a flaming sheet of debris. An angry cloud of smoke billows toward heaven: hardly how I envisioned entering Sin City. Nothing seems to go my way. Some moments are better than others. Probably sums up a Vegas vacation as well as any. Hiding outside behind a beat-up Chevy Citation in the furnace-heat of the Excalibur Casino's parking lot doesn't fall into the better moment category. Feel feverish and thirsty as I kneel behind the car and try to catch my breath. No time to rest, though. The cannibals, or zombies, are everywhere. I have to find some place to hide.

Acknowledgments

Original Library of the Living Dead Press Release Cover Art by Jodi Lee.

Want more?

Subscribe to **Beyond Apocalypse** newsletter to receive updates about Stephen Alexander North's writing.

Watch Book Trailers, Vlogs, and other videos on **YouTube**. Follow Stephen Alexander North on Social Media:

Facebook

Instagram

Pinterest

Twitter

Visit the **Beyond Apocalypse** Blog
For more stories by **Stephen Alexander North**
Thank you for your support of an Independent Author.
Sincerely,
Stephen Alexander North

Also By Stephen Alexander North - Amazon

Poetry

I Held the Sun

The Dark Joy for Despair

My Soul's on Fire

Prose

Forgotten

Nobody's Hero

Tusk

Undead in Vegas

<u>Dead Tide Rage</u>

<u>Beneath the Mask</u>

<u>The Drifter</u>

Barren Earth

About Stephen Alexander North:

Author Bio: Stephen Alexander North is a Florida native, a closet lounge singer, and the obscure Floridian writer of sci-fi, horror, thrillers, fantasy and poetry. He has a Bachelor of Arts in English Literature from the University of South Florida, and served as an Army Reservist.

Printed in Great Britain
by Amazon

45594529R00106